on a **day**
like
this

on a **day**
like
this *a novel*

PETER STAMM

Translated by
Michael Hofmann

OTHER PRESS · NEW YORK

We wish to express our appreciation to Pro Helvetia, Arts Council of Switzerland, for their assistance in the preparation of the translation.

swiss arts council
prohelvetia

Copyright © 2006 by Peter Stamm

Originally published in German as AN EINEM TAG WIE DIESEM by S. Fischer Verlag GmbH, Frankfurt am Main, 2006.

Translation copyright © 2007 Michael Hofmann

Production Editor: Yvonne E. Cárdenas

Text design: Natalya Balnova
This book was set in 11.2 pt AGaramond by Alpha Graphics of Pittsfield, NH.

10 9 8 7 6 5 4 3 2 1

Library of Congress Cataloging-in-Publication Data

Stamm, Peter, 1963-
    [An einem Tag wie diesem. English]
    On a day like this / Peter Stamm ; translated by Michael Hofmann.
        p. cm.
    ISBN-13: 978-1-59051-279-1
    I. Hofmann, Michael, 1957 Aug. 25- II. Title.
    PT2681.T3234A6613 2007
    833'.914—dc22
                                                            2007035108

*It is on a day like this, a little later, a little earlier,
that everything will start over, that everything will begin,
that everything will go on as before.*

—Georges Perec, *Un homme qui dort* (*A Man Asleep*)

Andreas loved the empty mornings when he would stand by the window with a cup of coffee in one hand and a cigarette in the other, and stare down at the small, tidy courtyard, and think about nothing except what was there in front of him: a small rectangular bed in the middle of the courtyard, planted with ivy with a tree in it, that put out a few thin branches, pruned to fit the small space that was available; the shiny green containers for glass, packing material, other rubbish; the even pattern of the cement paving blocks, some of which were a little lighter, having been replaced some years back for some unknown reason. The noise of the city was only faintly audible, reduced to an even roar, interspersed with distant bird-calls and the rather clearer noise of a window being opened and shut.

This unthinking state only lasted for a few minutes. Even before Andreas had finished his cigarette, he remembered last night. What did emptiness mean to him, Nadia had wanted to know. For her it meant lack of attention, lack of love, the absence of people she had lost, or who paid her insufficient attention. Emptiness was a space that had once been filled, or that she thought might be filled, the absence of something she couldn't put her finger on. He didn't know about that, Andreas had said, he wasn't interested in abstract notions.

Evenings with Nadia always followed the same pattern. She would arrive half an hour late, and give Andreas the feeling that it was he who was late. She would be wearing full makeup, and a short, tight skirt and black fishnet tights. She would drop her coat theatrically on the floor, sit down on the sofa, and cross her legs. As far as she was concerned, that was the high point of the evening, her entrance. She put a cigarette in her mouth, and Andreas gave her a light, and complimented her on her appearance. He went into the kitchen and came back with two glasses of wine. Nadia must have had something to drink already, she was a little bit excitable.

Usually, they ate in a local restaurant. The food wasn't bad, and the gay waiter bantered with Nadia.

Sometimes, if the restaurant wasn't too busy, he sat down at their table with them. Nadia drank and talked too much, and together with the waiter made fun of Andreas's being a vegetarian, and the fact that he always ordered the same thing off the menu. He said he wasn't a vegetarian, he just didn't eat meat that often. By dessert, if not before, Nadia would have gotten onto politics. She worked for a PR company. One of her clients was a group connected to the Socialist Party, whose views she represented in a way that drove Andreas crazy. By that point, he would often have stopped speaking, and she would ask him in an aggressive undertone if she bored him.

"I bore you," she said.

No, he said, but he was a foreigner, he didn't understand French politics, and wasn't that interested either. He obeyed the law, he sorted his trash, he taught the syllabus. Apart from that, he just wanted to be left in peace. Nadia would be annoyed by his lack of interest, and would lecture him, and they quarreled. Andreas tried to change the subject. Then every time Nadia would start to talk about her ex-husband, his lovelessness and his inattentiveness, Andreas got the feeling she was talking about him. Nadia couldn't stop complaining. She smoked one cigarette after another, and her voice got a little teary. All the other guests would have gone by then, and the waiter had emptied the ashtrays and wiped the espresso machine. When he came to their table and asked them if they wanted anything else, Nadia was suddenly a different person. She laughed and flirted with him, and that would go on for another fifteen minutes until Andreas was allowed to pay the bill.

On the way home, Nadia was quiet. They hadn't touched all evening. Now she linked arms with Andreas. He stopped in front of the building where he lived. He kissed her, first on the cheeks, then on the mouth. Sometimes he kissed her on the neck, and then he would feel a bit ridiculous. She seemed to like it, though. Presumably, it accorded with her own glamorous sense of herself. The sort of woman that men prostrated themselves in front of, who gets kissed on the neck, who laughs her lovers to scorn. Andreas would have liked to be alone now, but he asked her all the same if she wanted to come up. It sounded like capitulation.

Nadia was not one of those women who became more beautiful once you had slept with them. Her tight clothes were like a suit of armor; once she was naked she seemed to lose confidence, and looked old, older than she really was. She permitted everything to be done to her, enjoyed Andreas's caresses without reciprocating them. That—he should have said to her—was his idea of emptiness. These evenings with her, every other week, or rather the same evening over and over again, followed by the same night, and no sense of getting closer to her. But he didn't say anything. He enjoyed the sense that Nadia was somewhere else in her head, that she left him her body to do with as he pleased, then, after an hour or two, suddenly got impatient, shoved him away, and told him to call her a taxi. Emptiness meant those evenings with her, the afternoons with Sylvie, or the weekends by himself at home in his warm, comfortable apartment, where he would watch TV, play a computer game, or just read. Emptiness was his life in this city, the eighteen years in which nothing had changed, without his wishing for anything to change.

Emptiness was the normal state of things, he had said, nor was it anything he was afraid of—quite the opposite.

Sometimes, when Andreas crossed the street on his way to work, he imagined what it would be like to be run over by a bus. The collision would be the end of what had been thus far, and at the same time a sort of fresh start. A blow that would put an end to entanglements and create a little order. Suddenly, everything seemed significant, the date and the hour, the name of the street or boulevard, and that of the bus driver, even Andreas himself, the date and place of his birth, his profession, his religion. It was a rainy morning, winter or fall. The gleaming asphalt reflected the lights of the electric signs and the car headlights. The traffic piled up behind the bus, which blocked the road. An ambulance came. Pedestrians stood and gawked. A policeman waved the traffic past the site of the accident. The passengers in other buses craned their necks or stuck their heads out of the window. They failed to understand what had happened, or else forgot it straightaway when a different scene caught their attention. A second policeman came and tried to reconstruct the accident. He asked the bus driver, the woman in the bakery who had seen it all happen, a further witness. Then he would write up a report in duplicate, a file that would be stored in some archive somewhere, arranged in an alphabetical sequence of fatal accidents. Andreas imagined the measures that would have to be taken to remove him from the system. His brother would have to be informed, it would be for him to decide what would be done with the body. Andreas had withstood the temptation to draw up a will, it had always struck him as rather narcissistic to leave instructions in the event of one's own death. Presumably Walter would opt for incineration, that was the simplest and most sensible course. Even so, there would be a lot of paperwork to be done, and all sorts of official business. The embassy would certainly have to become involved.

Andreas asked himself whether a detailed account would be drawn up of the last working days before his death. The school authorities would know what to do. Perhaps there was even a memo somewhere listing the steps that had to be taken in the event of the unexpected death of foreign members of the teaching staff.

And then, after a few days of excitement, following letters and phone calls and *sotto voce* conversations in the staff room, there would be a modest funeral, a wreath from the school, a floral tribute from his colleagues. Walter would buy a big bouquet from the discount florist at the corner. He would have traveled up from Switzerland, found a cheap room somewhere in the neighborhood, and he would now be trying, with his bad French, to organize everything. He had got hold of Andreas's appointment and address book. There was insufficient time to place an announcement in the newspaper, but he would call some of Andreas's friends and invite them. He would be surprised by the number of women's names in the address book, perhaps he felt a bit jealous of his brother's bachelor existence. In the evenings he would call his wife and complain about the officiousness of the authorities, and ask how the children were doing. Then he would go out for a meal locally, and go for a walk in the rue des Abesses or the rue Pigalle. Andreas asked himself whether his brother might take in a peepshow or go with a prostitute. He couldn't imagine it.

From the Gare du Nord, Andreas took the suburban train out to Deuil-la-Barre. He took the same train every day. He studied the faces of the other passengers, ordinary, unremarkable faces. An elderly man sitting across from him stared at him with expressionless eyes. Andreas looked out the window. He saw rails, factories and storage facilities, an occasional tree, electricity towers or lampposts, brick or concrete walls spattered with graffiti. He had a sense of seeing only colors, ocher, yellow, white, silver, a dull red, and the watery blue of the sky. It was a little after seven, but time seemed not to matter.

He asked himself whether Walter would leave the clearing out of the apartment to a moving company. The furniture hadn't been exactly cheap, but what use would he have for it? That aside, Andreas didn't have many possessions. Personal effects—he had always asked himself what that meant. A little statuette of Diana with bow and arrow, frozen in mid-step, that he had bought at a flea market shortly after his arrival in Paris, a couple of posters from art exhibits long ago, and framed vacation photos of deserted landscapes in the dazzling heat of Italy and the South of France. He owned hardly any books, a few CDs and DVDs, nothing special, nothing of value. His clothes and his shoes wouldn't fit Walter, who was bigger and bulkier than he was. The apartment itself was the only thing that could be turned into cash. Andreas had bought it at a time when the neighborhood wasn't as sought-after as it was now.

It was a strange thing that his brother, with whom he had so little in common and whom he didn't even resemble, was the person who would have to deal with all this. Andreas didn't like to think his death would put anyone to any trouble. But probably that was unavoidable.

He looked around at the other passengers, a pair of lovers kissing by the door, two children whispering, old women with tired faces, businessmen in cheap shiny suits, reading the business section of the paper with grave expressions on their faces. In a hundred years you'll all be dead, he thought to himself. The sun would shine, the trains would move, children would go to school, but he and all the other people traveling with him today would be dead, and along with them, this moment, this journey, as though it had never been.

The passengers who got off the train with Andreas seemed to be different every day. He stopped on the platform for a moment and watched as they dispersed in all directions. Even though it was still cool, he took off his jacket. He felt a chill, but he loved the cool of the morning, which felt like a superficial caress.

He used to teach in a suburb that was even further out. He had always applied for jobs in the city, but every time he had lost out to colleagues who were older or who were married or had children. Ten years ago, when they built the secondary school at Deuil, Andreas gave up his dream of a job in the city. At least he didn't have so far to go to work as before.

He was always there half an hour before the beginning of classes. The staff room smelled of cigarettes, even though smoking was not permitted anywhere in the school. Andreas got coffee from the machine and sat down by the window. After about fifteen minutes, Jean-

Marc came in, one of the gym teachers. He was wearing a tracksuit.

"Have you been smoking?" he asked, as he washed his face in the sink. Andreas said nothing.

"I can't believe you're allowed to smoke in staff rooms in Switzerland."

Andreas said he hadn't been in a staff room anywhere in Switzerland for a very long time.

"Can I ask you a personal question?" said Jean-Marc.

"I'd rather you didn't."

Jean-Marc laughed. He had pulled off his tracksuit top, and was washing his armpits. He said it was too bad they hadn't installed a shower for the teachers. He squirted on a deodorant, the smell of it spread through the room. Jean-Marc got dressed again. He got a glass of water, and sat down right next to Andreas.

"You must know Delphine?" he leaned back with a smug expression. "What do you think of her?"

"She's nice," said Andreas. "There's something refreshing about her."

"That's exactly it."

Andreas went over to the window, opened it, and lit a cigarette. Jean-Marc gave him a glare.

"We went for a drink together," he said, "and somehow I ended up staying with her."

"And what's that to do with me?"

"Well, since then she's pretended nothing happened. As though she didn't know me."

"You should be pleased. Do you want her calling you at home?"

Jean-Marc stood up and raised his hands. "God, no," he said, "but it's strange. You sleep with a woman, someone . . . not even beautiful. Did that ever happen to you?"

"I'm not married," said Andreas. It seemed grotesque to him that he would certainly have described Jean-Marc as his best friend.

After Andreas turned off the light at night, he lay awake a little. He had drawn the curtains, and the only light in the darkened room was from the TV, the DVD player, and the stereo. The red luminous diodes had something calming about them, they reminded him of the light that doesn't go out, of the presence of Christ, whom he didn't believe in.

He spent Saturday as always, cleaning the apartment, and shopping for the week ahead. Some years ago, a film that had achieved cult status had been shot in the street, and since that time people came there from all over the world to check out the reality of the dream scenes. Andreas had bought a DVD of the film, and when he watched it from time to time, it seemed to him the pictures were more real than the street outside, as though the reality were just a pale imitation of the silvery film world, a cheap stage set. You had to close your eyes to hear the soundtrack and see the images. Then Paris was the way he had always imagined it.

Andreas liked being part of this stage set. He liked the sense he had of himself sitting in a café reading the newspaper, or strolling down the street with a baguette under his arm, and carrying bags full of vegetables that would spend the week rotting in his fridge before he threw them away. When tourists stopped him and asked for directions, he was only too glad to tell them. He answered them in French, even when he noticed they were German or Swiss and had trouble understanding him.

He was both an extra in the imaginary film and a member of the audience, a tourist who had walked these streets for twenty years now, without ever having a sense of arriving anywhere. He was quite happy with his part, he had never wanted to be anything else.

Great undertakings and major changes had always alarmed him. He walked through the streets of St. Michel or St. Germain, went up the Eiffel Tower, or took a look around the church of Notre Dame or the Louvre. He strolled across the Pont Neuf and went shopping in the big stores, even though the prices were ridiculous. Sometimes he would follow people on the street for a while, see what they bought or watched them stop in a café for a drink, and then he let them go. When he talked to friends who had spent all their lives in Paris, he was amazed by how poorly they knew the city. They barely left their *quartier*, and hadn't visited the museums since their school days. Instead of rejoicing in the city's beauty, they complained about the striking Metro workers, the polluted air, and the lack of parks and playgrounds.

Late in the afternoon, he would go to the cinema and watch an American action film, some routine story with spectacular stunts and special effects. On his way home, he would be accosted by the doormen at the sex clubs. Previously, they had always been rather slimy young men, but for some time now they were women, who were even more persistent than men. Andreas looked straight ahead and waved them away with his hand, but one of the women followed him as far as the next traffic light, talking to him, and saying, well, how about it, come on in. We have new girls.

"I live here," he said, and crossed the street against the red light, to get rid of the woman.

It annoyed him that he was always accosted. It was as though they could see through his disguise, as though they knew something about him that he didn't know himself. Life must be pretty hard behind the scenes, behind the blacked-out doors of the sex clubs and bars and sex shops. The thought that that life might be more real than his own upset him. In all the years he had lived there, he had never once gone to one of those places.

He slept in on Sundays. He ate breakfast in a café, read the newspaper, and listened to a young German couple argue about their plans for the rest of the day. She wanted to go to the Louvre; he didn't. When she asked what he wanted to do instead, he had no suggestions.

At twelve o'clock, Andreas was back home. He corrected a batch of homework, then he leafed through a couple of little books he'd picked up on Friday in the German-language bookstore. They were part of a series of instruction books that he sometimes read with the more advanced pupils, little thriller texts about art thieves or smuggler bands, written in simple vocabulary of six or twelve or eighteen hundred words, that was somehow enough to describe an entire world. Andreas liked the stories, even though they were incredibly banal and predictable.

He quickly laid aside the first volume. It was about ecoterrorism, a subject that depressed him, and seemed to him unsuitable for his pupils. The second was titled *Love Without Borders*. On the cover, it had a line-drawing that reminded him of the Sixties, and that he found strangely moving: a young couple sitting at a sidewalk café under tall trees, smiling at one another. Andreas read the jacket copy. The story was about a girl from Paris called Angélique, who takes a job as an au pair in Germany, and falls in love with Jens, a marine biology student. The host family live in Rendsburg, up near the Danish border. Many years before, Andreas had attended a conference there once, on Scandinavian literature. He had liked the town, even though it had rained the whole time, and he hardly saw anything of the countryside.

He didn't like reading love stories with the kids. Every kiss was accompanied by giggles and whispers and stupid remarks. But when he was younger, he had fallen in love with an au pair himself. He began reading.

I couldn't concentrate on the traffic. I had to keep looking at her. The Volkswagen smelled of her, and of summer, sun, and fields of flowers.

Andreas thought about Fabienne, and going swimming with her and Manuel in the lake. He had gone to school with Manuel, and later, while they were both away at college, they sometimes ran into each other on the train home. Andreas was studying German and French, Manuel was qualifying as a gym teacher. He owned an ancient 2CV that was always breaking down.

Fabienne and Andreas was a love story that had never quite happened. He had been in love with her all right, but he had never been sure where she stood. One summer, they had met almost every day, had spent a lot of time together, but he had never dared to declare his love to her, and Fabienne seemed not to expect such a declaration from him. When he was already living in Paris, he wrote her a letter where he finally talked about his feelings; he never sent it.

Andreas hadn't thought about Fabienne or Manuel for a long time. He hadn't heard anything from them for ages. He had a vague recollection of a birth announcement, a bland baby face, with the weight and height of a newborn, as though that meant anything.

Presumably he had offered his congratulations, maybe sent a gift, he couldn't remember anymore. He had seen the two of them again, briefly, at his father's funeral, and not since.

He turned over a couple of pages.

I took her hand and kissed it. Shortly afterward, we were lying on the canal bank.

"You are an amazing person. How can I understand you?"

"You're not to understand me, Butterfly," I replied, and looked at her. "I don't understand myself. Often I don't even know what I want, you see."

"Too bad," she said quietly. "It would be nice if you knew what I felt like now."

For the next twenty minutes, neither of us spoke much. When we got up, Angélique brushed the grass off her pants.

"I like you."

"You're sweet."

Andreas stared at the book. Butterfly was what he had sometimes called Fabienne, in English, because her German then was as bad as his French. And she had said he didn't know what he wanted, in her over-distinct pronunciation. *You do not know what you want.*

He remembered the scene. It was a hot day. The three of them had driven out to the lake. They changed into their bathing suits in the undergrowth. Manuel said he would swim to the other side, and disappeared. Fabienne was sunbathing on her back, eyes closed. Andreas remembered her ivory-colored bathing suit, and that she had put her hair up. He looked at her, and then he bent down over her. She must have felt his shadow cross her face. She opened her eyes and looked at him.

He kissed her, and she let it happen. He laid his hand on her throat, caressed her shoulder, and gently brushed over her bosom. Then she broke free, and ran down to the lake.

Andreas stayed lying there for a while. He was stunned that he had actually dared to kiss Fabienne. He dived into the water, and set off after her. Fabienne swam slowly, head out of the water in an effort to keep her hair dry. Andreas had to hang back if he wasn't to pass her. After a while, Manuel swam out to meet them. They turned back with him, and returned to their spot on the bank.

Later, Manuel tried to teach Fabienne the butterfly. In the past semester he had learned all the various swimming styles, and he showed off his expertise. Perhaps that was why Andreas had started calling her Butterfly. Or was it Manuel who had started that? Suddenly Andreas didn't feel sure.

Manuel stood next to Fabienne in the shallow water, and tried to grab her by the waist, but she took a couple of quick steps away from him, and gave him the slip. Manuel set off after her. When he didn't catch her, he splashed water at her, and she ran to the bank.

They had stayed by the lake for a long time that day. When it got dark, they lit a fire. Manuel started to talk about religion in his bad English, and Fabienne argued with him. She was Catholic and couldn't deal with his Protestant views, his love of Jesus, who, the way he talked about him, sounded like a good friend. Andreas played the nihilist. He got excited. Now it was his turn to show off with glib remarks on the futility of human existence. In the end, Manuel and Fabienne joined forces against him, and he hurled accusations at them that he later regretted. He looked at Fabienne and tried to read some lingering trace of his kiss in her eyes. But all he saw in her look was distaste.

On the way home, she sat in the front, next to Manuel. It was a warm night, they had the roof of the 2CV down, as they drove back over the hill to the village. Manuel drew up in front of Andreas's parents' house. They said their good-byes. Fabienne leaned back between the seats and kissed Andreas on both cheeks. He stopped by the garden gate and watched the car disappear around the corner. Then he remained sitting on the front steps for a long time, smoking and thinking about Fabienne and his love for her.

When he next saw her, a couple of days later, she was different, still friendly but distant. They went swimming again, but Fabienne seemed to take care not to be alone with Andreas. Eventually the weather changed, and it got too cold to swim. Then they only saw each other with the rest of the group, going to the cinema or meeting in a restaurant. In the autumn, Fabienne returned to Paris, to study German. Andreas hadn't gone to the station to see her off—why, he could no longer remember.

After Fabienne was gone, Andreas felt how little he and Manuel had in common. They saw each other once or twice still, but without Fabienne there, their meetings were boring.

He read the scene a second time. The footnotes explained those words that were not part of the basic vocabulary.

canal: man-made waterway
alongside: next to, by the side of
kiss: two people pressing their lips together

At the end of the chapter there were some comprehension questions.

Why is Jens disappointed?
What do you know about Angélique?
Where is Schleswig-Holstein?

That time at the lake, Andreas felt glad that Fabienne had run away. He was in love with her, but for the time being that first kiss was enough for him, that first touch. In the ensuing weeks he sometimes imagined what would have happened if she had kissed him back. They would run into the forest together. They would hide in the undergrowth, take off their bathing suits. They would lie on the forest floor, which was warm and soft in Andreas's imagination. Then Manuel would come calling for them, and they would hurriedly pull their bathing suits back on and stroll down to the lake, as though nothing had happened. Fabienne would look at Andreas, and smile. Manuel surely must have noticed what had happened, but Andreas didn't care. In his imagination he felt strangely proud and solemn. They were all quiet on the drive back. Andreas sat in the back, studying Fabienne, her tanned neck, with little tiny, almost invisible hairs on it, her pink translucent ears, her pinned back hair. Through her T-shirt he could see the outline of her shoulderblades and the straps of her bra.

Fabienne's beauty had always taken his breath away. It was the flawless beauty of a statue. He imagined his hands gliding over her body, which would be cool as bronze or smooth marble. In his projection, Fabienne had remained the young girl he had first met, and when he thought of her he felt as young and inexperienced as he had been at the time. He couldn't imagine Fabienne sweaty or tired, or aroused, or in a temper. He couldn't imagine her naked.

In the winter after Fabienne's departure, Andreas's mother died of breast cancer. She had known she was sick for some time, but she had first concealed it from the family, and then played it down. Even when she had only a little time to live, she still pretended everything was OK. The atmosphere in the house was unbearable, and finally Andreas rented a room in the city, and came home only at weekends. He would usually arrive after lunch on Saturday, and go straight up to his room. He said he had to work. Then he would lie on his bed and read his old children's books, and only come down for supper. After supper, he disappeared as quickly as possible into the village, to meet friends. He drank too much, and when he came home late at night, drunk, he would sometimes run into his mother, who was unable to sleep. She was standing in the kitchen, swallowing some homeopathic remedy that she tried to keep him from seeing. She would say good night, and pad down the dark corridor to her bedroom, but, once Andreas was in bed, he could hear her getting up again and restlessly pacing about the house.

In those months he started going out with Manuel's younger sister, Beatrice, who worked as a teller at the Canton Bank, and had just broken up with her boyfriend. The relationship lasted just six months. Beatrice was still living with her parents, who were religious people and wouldn't have allowed Andreas to spend the night with their daughter. Sometimes, Beatrice visited him in the city, but she never wanted to stay over. Andreas said she was legal, but she shook her head and said, no, she couldn't do that to her parents. She let him undress her to her underwear, then she said she wasn't ready yet, she wanted to get to know him a bit better first. Even when she touched him, Andreas thought she didn't really want to, and it was just to please him. Eventually he had enough. He called her at the bank and said he didn't want to see her anymore. She said she was working, and wasn't able to talk, and he said there was nothing to talk about, and hung up. After that he didn't answer the phone for a week. He saw Beatrice at his mother's funeral. She had come with Manuel. The two of them offered him their condolences, and they exchanged a few meaningless sentences. Years later, Andreas heard that Beatrice had got back together with her ex, and married him.

During his time with Beatrice, he started writing letters to Fabienne. He had thought about her a lot after her going away, and sometimes when he was lying on the bed with Beatrice, he shut his eyes and imagined it was Fabienne beside him. From that time, she had accompanied him through all his relationships. She was always there, as a shadow, fading a little over time, but never quite disappearing.

Andreas went into the kitchen to make some tea. Then he lay down on the sofa, and started reading the little book from the beginning.

The love between Angélique and Jens was almost as chaste as that between him and Fabienne. Sex did not play any part in the basic vocabulary, and Jens appeared more interested in the beauty of Schleswig-Holstein than in Angélique's. He drove her around the area in his old Beetle, showed her the Viking museum at Haithabu and the famous Bordesholm altar in Schleswig, and walked along the North Sea-Baltic Canal with her, one of the most important waterways of the world, as he explained to her. He kissed her for the first time on the Rendsburg ferry, and then they went on excursions even further afield. A visit to Lübeck gave Jens the opportunity to deliver himself of the stupidest sentence on Thomas Mann that Andreas had ever read. He turned over a few pages, and it was fall. The date of Angélique's departure was moving nearer, casting its dark shadow on the young happiness. Just as Jens was on his way to the station to say good-bye to Angélique, and promise to visit her in Paris, his car developed another problem, and by the time he finally got to the station, all he could see of her train were its two taillights. Foolishly, the two of them hadn't even exchanged addresses, and for a couple of pages it looked as if they would never see each other again. But then Jens managed to get a place to study in Paris. In the spring, he set off after Angélique, and only a few days later, by a wildly improbable coincidence, he met her strolling down the Champs-Elysées. A happy ending in spring light, a jerky pen-and-ink sketch of bliss.

The story was implausible and badly written, but it had extraordinary parallels to Andreas's own. He too had set off in pursuit of Fabienne, though only after two years. They had exchanged letters that whole time. Andreas had never referred explicitly to the kiss by the lake, but his letters had been full of hints. Fabienne must have sensed what he felt for her.

She was never the first to write, but she replied to all his letters. She wrote about her studies, her family, her friends. She did not mention that Manuel had come to visit her in Paris, just as she did not mention her trips to Switzerland. Not until Andreas had finished his degree and got an assistantship in a school on the outskirts of Paris did she tell him, in a postscript, that she would be going to Switzerland in October. She and Manuel were an item, and all the to-ing and fro-ing had gotten a bit wearing, and a bit expensive as well.

Andreas was stunned. He asked himself why he had never thought to visit Fabienne. He thought of turning down the job, but then he went there anyway. He resolved to speak to Fabienne. For weeks he thought about what he would say to her. He couldn't imagine what she saw in Manuel, who had just taken a job as a gym teacher in the village where he and Andreas had grown up.

No sooner had he got to Paris than he called Fabienne. She said she was very busy, she was sitting her exams. They ended up arranging to meet on one of the following days in the tearoom of the mosque.

In the two years they hadn't seen each other, Fabienne had grown still more beautiful. She had lost some weight, and her features were clearer, more mature. She looked utterly self-possessed, walking across the crowded café to greet Andreas, ordering mint tea and pastries for them. Andreas talked about his job, his pupils, and his new colleagues. Fabienne talked about her exams, which had gone well, about her summer vacation, about the books she had read. She said she was going to Zürich to finish her degree. Her German was still not good, she badly needed to spend time in a German-speaking environment. Andreas said she didn't have the trace of an accent, and anyway Switzerland was the last place she should go to for that. Fabienne just laughed. He didn't say what he had meant to say. After an hour, Fabienne got up and said she had to go, she was due to meet a girlfriend.

In the two months that Fabienne remained in Paris, they met four or five times. They drank tea or coffee, and once they went to the cinema to see a Fritz Lang film. Just before the end, the film tore, and after a long pause the house lights came on, and a woman walked to the front and said that for technical reasons they were unable to show the ending of the film. In a few sentences she told them how the story ended.

Andreas asked Fabienne to have a drink with him. She was tired, she said. He walked her back to her place. The whole evening they had spoken only banalities. As they walked along side by side, he wanted to say at last the things he had wanted to say, but he couldn't get a syllable out, only a wheeze. Fabienne asked if he had said something. No, he said, it was just a frog in his throat.

Andreas never supposed that falling in love with an au pair was a particularly original thing to do. It had probably happened lots of times. But what was striking were the many details of his story that chimed with the book. The nickname he had given Fabienne, her appearance, the fact that she had bought herself a cat in Paris, and liked seeing old German films. That she sang him French nursery rhymes, and that her father was a doctor.

The author of the little book was named Gregor Wolf. There was a little biographical sketch of him at the front of the book. Apparently, he was born in 1953, and after training to be a bookseller, he had done various jobs, among them waiter and night porter. He had lived abroad for a long time. As of 1985, he was a freelance writer, living in Flensburg and Majorca. The biography sounded like every other author biography. Andreas had never heard of him, but that didn't mean much. At the back of the book was a list of other books by Gregor Wolf, and there followed a dozen or so catchpenny titles.

Andreas asked himself whether Fabienne had ever met the author, and told him her story. It seemed unlikely, but what was even more unlikely was that all the coincidences were accidental.

He put the book down and turned on the TV to catch the news. Afterward he switched it off. The programs that would have interested him were generally on too late. He went to bed early, and was soon asleep. When the alarm went off, he still felt tired. He went to the bathroom, cleaned his teeth, and showered, first hot then cold. He didn't eat any breakfast, just gulped down a cup of coffee, and set off.

On Wednesday, Andreas met Sylvie. They always arranged to meet on afternoons of no school, but other things often got in the way. Sylvie had three children, and when one of them was ill, or had a music lesson canceled, she would send him a text message to cancel their meeting. When they did meet, she would always make a joke about their relationship. Sometimes Andreas suspected she had other lovers besides him, but he never asked. He thought it was none of his business, and in fact he didn't care either way.

Sylvie would arrive on her bicycle. She was out of breath when she walked past him into the apartment. He asked if she wanted a drink, but she said she didn't have much time, put her arms around him, and dragged him into the bedroom.

Once they had slept together, Sylvie was a little calmer. She talked about her husband and her children, and the little catastrophes that always seemed to befall her. She had numerous relatives and close friends who always seemed to need her help, and Andreas listened to her, and got the people she talked about all mixed up. She only ever used first names. That's your brother, right? asked Andreas. No, said Sylvie, with a show of irritation, he's my best friend's husband, or my husband's cousin, or Anne's French teacher. Sometimes Sylvie asked him why he never talked. He said he had nothing to say. His life was too formless, and at the same time too much of a tangle to give rise to any stories. Sylvie didn't listen. She stood by the window looking out. She was naked, but she behaved quite as if she were dressed.

"What a horrible yard," she said. "What kind of people live here?"

"I've hardly met any of the neighbors."

"How long have you lived in this building?"

Andreas figured it out.

"Almost ten years," he said.

Sylvie laughed and returned to bed. She kissed him on the mouth. Andreas grabbed her around the waist, and pulled her down. Sylvie sat up.

"Now you can offer me a drink, if you like."

Andreas put on his pants, and went into the kitchen to make coffee. Sylvie followed him. She said she didn't understand how he could stand to live in such a tiny apartment.

"I can't afford a bigger one."

"I've got some friends in Belleville who want to sell their apartment. It's three big rooms, and not expensive. I'm sure you'd get four hundred thousand for yours. The area's become so fashionable."

Andreas said the apartment wasn't as small as all that. And he felt at home in it. He didn't need any more space. Then he told Sylvie about Angélique and Jens, and his love for Fabienne.

"It's the exact same story," he said. "Isn't that amazing."

"But your version of it ended badly."

"Yes, for me," said Andreas. He handed Sylvie a cup, and sat down on the kitchen table. "Maybe she met the author. He lives on Majorca. Stranger things have happened."

"Then why should she tell him the story with a happy ending?"

"I've no idea," said Andreas.

"Perhaps she was in love with you. Perhaps she wanted it to end well."

"I was an idiot," said Andreas.

Sylvie asked what was special about Fabienne. Andreas said she was very beautiful when he first met her. But that couldn't be the whole story. If he met Fabienne now, he would still find her attractive, maybe he would approach her, have an affair with her. She wouldn't be the great love of his life, not now, not anymore. Presumably it wasn't even Fabienne herself that he longed for, so much as the love of those years, the unconditionality of the feeling that still floored him now, twenty years later.

"The bull that's led to the cow probably thinks he's in love too," said Sylvie, and laughed. She said she'd better go, and went into the bedroom to get dressed.

"Write to her," she said, as she said good-bye.

Andreas had decided to write to Fabienne, but he kept putting it off and putting it off, until he finally forgot all about it. There was some trouble at school, a couple of pupils started a fight during recess. One of them was in Andreas's class, and there were meetings with the headmistress and the parents and a social worker. Then a letter came from Walter. Andreas was very surprised to hear from Walter. They talked on the phone every other month or so, and never had very much to say to each other. Sometimes Walter would send him a post-card from his vacation, which they would all sign, and at Christmas there was a round-robin letter containing all the news of the past year; apart from that, they never wrote to each other. The letter was accompanied by a form. *Clearing of a grave*, Andreas read. Under that heading were the names of his parents, handwritten, and under the heading, *Client*, was Walter's name and his own.

> *The undersigned client is prepared to meet the expenses of the cemetery gardener in the removal of the grave. The leveling and refurbishment of the grave space will be paid for by the community.*

Walter had signed the form. Normal practice was for graves to be given up after twenty years, he wrote in his accompanying letter, but the grave counted as that of their mother only. When their father was cremated, they had signed a disclaimer of burial rights, perhaps Andreas remembered. He was sorry to bother him over something like this, but he hadn't wanted to make the decision on his own. He had thought Andreas might want to visit the grave once more. It wouldn't be cleared until fall at the earliest. If he did decide to come to Switzerland, he would of course be welcome to stay with them. They would be pleased to see him again. Walter had signed the letter as "Your Brother," which struck Andreas as being in poor taste.

He remembered his father's funeral. It was a hot day. At that time, Walter and his family had still lived in an apartment, and Andreas had refused their offer of spending the night there. He had booked a room in the hotel on the market square. Walter had asked whether he wanted to be picked up in the morning, but Andreas said he didn't want to put him to any trouble.

During that whole stay, he had had the feeling of being in a kind of trance. The simplest decisions had been incredibly difficult for him, and he was only able to think about absolutely insignificant things. But his physical awareness had been strangely heightened. Everything seemed to him unbearably loud and intense. Colors, sounds, even smells were more vivid than usual. When he crossed the road to the cemetery, a car braked, and the driver lowered his window and yelled at him. Andreas walked on, not turning around. He felt a trickle of sweat break out on his brow and down his back.

There were a couple of cars in the cemetery parking lot, but no one to be seen. The heavy wrought-iron gate lay in the shadow of heavy conifers. Andreas had his suitcase with him; he intended to leave right after the funeral. Now he didn't know what to do with his suitcase. He thought briefly of shoving it in some bushes near the entrance to the cemetery, but rejected the idea immediately. He took off his jacket and lit a cigarette.

His shirt was sodden with sweat. A breeze cooled the wet cotton on his back and under his arms.

The funeral party was standing in little groups outside the chapel, engaged in quiet conversation. There were a lot of his old school friends there. They nodded to him as he walked by, one or another of them muttered something, asked him how he was doing, and what his plans were. Andreas looked around for Walter, but couldn't see him anywhere.

With a surprisingly loud clang, the church bells started to ring on the other side of the road, and the funeral party moved with slow, reverent steps to the entrance of the chapel. The situation struck Andreas as grotesque, the grave expressions, the whispering, the embarrassment. His father had been old, he had lived a retired sort of life, and Andreas was sure most of the people here had barely known him.

He stopped outside the chapel. When the bells ceased, and the sexton emerged from the chapel door to look around for any latecomers, Walter and his wife came out of one of the lying-in rooms, which were all housed in a low, long annex. Walter looked more surprised than grieving. He looked nervously at his watch. Bettina's face was tear-stained.

They hadn't seen Andreas. He followed them into the chapel. He was still holding his cigarette butt in his hand. It occurred to him to drop it in the holy water basin by the entrance. He stood his suitcase on the floor and leaned against the back wall.

Walter and Bettina walked down the nave. They took their places in the front row, where Bettina's parents were already sitting, and the children. The children were all dressed in colors. Presumably that was Bettina's idea. When Walter sat down, he half-turned his head, and the movement became a sort of bow, as though he wanted to greet the mourners. He smiled sheepishly. At that moment, Andreas felt sorry for him, and he would have liked to go up to him and give him a hug.

Walter lowered his head. The children slithered about, bored. Then the organ began, the mourners relaxed, and settled into their pews.

Only then did Andreas see Fabienne and Manuel. They were sitting in a row near the back, not far from him. As Fabienne leaned over to Manuel to whisper something in his ear, Andreas could see her profile. She had hardly changed at all. She was wearing a sleeveless black dress. Andreas wished he could touch her shoulders and her neck. Manuel was wearing a dark suit. He had lost a lot of hair, and had gotten rather chubby. As a young man he had been good-looking in a not particularly interesting sort of way; now he looked old to Andreas, though they were the same age.

The vicar seemed to be suffering from the heat. He was pale, and rattled through his sermon and a fairly interchangeable vita of the deceased, that was all work and births of children and memberships of clubs. Some of it Andreas had never heard of—or forgotten it. The little he did know he had heard from his mother.

The lady organist played a couple of wrong notes. Andreas was glad there wasn't any singing. For the prayers he put his hands together without folding them. He dropped the cigarette butt quietly on the floor. He didn't close his eyes, and as he looked at the swaying figures of those praying, he didn't know who was more ridiculous—the others in their adherence to a meaningless ritual or himself in his pose of rebellion.

During the service, the coffin had been brought out into the churchyard. It now stood there, but no one seemed to be paying it any attention. Andreas couldn't imagine that the dead man had anything to do with him. His father had been a quiet and reserved man. If he had still been alive, he would probably have stood on the periphery somewhere, in the shade of one of the pines, and observed the gathering with a nervous and at the same time amused eye. Andreas felt no grief at the time. Grief came later, when he was back in Paris, in his customary surroundings, and with a violence that had taken him aback.

Walter went up to Andreas, shook hands, and took him to his family. Bettina's face had a somehow complicated look on it; she resembled an old woman. They said hello, and then the vicar came up to them and said something comforting, and the mourners got in line to offer their condolences. All of them looked bashful and did their best to make their grief appear genuine. Walter's face had the startled expression it had had before, and sometimes, when he was shaking hands with someone, a forced cheerfulness.

Fabienne and Manuel came along right at the end. By the time it was their turn, the first mourners had already left the cemetery. Manuel shook Andreas's hand with an encouraging-looking smile.

"Glad we could see each other again," he said, rather too loudly.

Fabienne stood next to him. Andreas looked at her. She smiled, and once again he longed to touch her.

"Your father was a nice man," she said. She spoke correct German, her accent was barely detectable.

Andreas kissed her on both cheeks, and asked whether she and Manuel would stay to eat with them. He turned to Walter, and asked where the wake was being held. Manuel said unfortunately they wouldn't be able to stay. His mother was babysitting the boy. They had to be back for lunch. He laughed for no reason. Fabienne asked whether Andreas was staying for any length of time. Why didn't he come and visit them. She looked at him expectantly. When Andreas said he was going back today, he thought he saw disappointment flash across her face. But he wasn't sure. Fabienne had composed herself again. She said he hadn't changed at all.

"Come and see us the next time you're in the country," she said. "We'd like that." But it didn't sound like an invitation.

"Definitely," said Andreas. He was annoyed with Fabienne for talking of we and us, and not I.

After the funeral meal, he went back briefly to Walter and Bettina's place. The wine and the heat had made him tired. It was cool in the apartment. They sat in the sitting room, talking about their father. Walter showed Andreas a stack of old school notebooks. The square paper was divided into vertical columns of dates and numbers.

"You know he kept a record of the temperature each day, highs and lows, plus the humidity and pressure. Always at the same time of day. An endless list. He did it for forty years."

Andreas said the notebooks seemed familiar. He had never quite understood what his father did it for.

"He stopped a couple of weeks before he died," said Walter, suddenly bursting into sobs. Andreas couldn't recall ever having seen him cry before, and felt embarrassed.

Walter had taken care of everything, the cremation, the thanking people, the execution of the will. Andreas had been sent the papers, and signed without reading them. Then Walter and his family moved into their parents' house, and paid Andreas his share. That was the money he had bought the Paris apartment with. He had been to Switzerland a couple of times since, but never the village.

The thought that the grave was being cleared bothered him. For a moment he thought of going. Then he signed the form and put it in an envelope. He looked for an appropriate postcard. Finally he selected a Gauguin of a Breton village in warm colors. He wrote to say that unfortunately he didn't have any time to visit Switzerland. He sent his love and best wishes to the family. He mailed the letter right away. He wanted to be free of the matter.

Andreas met Nadia and Sylvie, he did the shopping, he cleaned the apartment, he went to the cinema. The kids at school were difficult, and for the first time in many years, Andreas derived no satisfaction from his job. When the class complained to him about a test, he lectured them. Did they really think he did all that just to give them a hard time? He was doing it for them. He had a syllabus and goals. He hadn't chosen his profession by chance; he was a teacher by vocation. He said he believed that education made people better. And that as long as they were in school, they had a chance to learn something, while other people had to spend their whole lives doing some stupid job. Knowledge of German would open doors for them, intellectually speaking, especially philosophy, which one couldn't hope to understand without learning German. German was the language of philosophy, it had a clarity and purity that no other language could claim to have, and at the same time . . .

The longer he went on, the more hollow his words sounded to him. He looked at the kids slumped across their desks and whispering and giggling and trying to avoid his eye. He broke off in mid-sentence and sat down.

From that day forward, he saw the students with different eyes. He no longer deluded himself that he had any influence on them. Even the good boys and the eager girls who tried hard, who did their homework diligently and participated in the classes, annoyed him. They reminded him of himself, and of what had become of him.

He no longer enjoyed going to school. He suffered from the monotony of his days and felt tired and burned out. In the staff room there were endless discussions about the banning of head-scarves, even though there were no Muslim girls in the school, and head-scarves had never been an issue. The teachers formed two opposing camps. Andreas wanted to belong to neither one. It seemed to him they were both merely trying to settle old accounts. In Switzerland, he once heard himself saying, they dealt with these problems more calmly. After that, he was attacked by both sides, one called him racist, the other misogynist. Even Jean-Marc had come across all political, and defended the values of the republic that he seemed barely to have acknowledged before.

Andreas spent his spring break in Normandy. Once again, he had intended to read Proust, but he ended up sitting around in the hotel, watching TV or reading the newspapers and magazines he bought at the station newsstand every morning. He spent a night with an unmarried woman teacher he had met on one of his long walks along the beach. He had been fascinated by her large breasts, and invited her to supper. It took a lot of effort to talk her into going up to his room, and then they talked for a lot longer while they emptied the minibar. While they made love, the woman kept moaning his name out loud, which got on his nerves. He was glad to be alone when he woke up late the following morning. She had left him a note, which he glanced at briefly before balling it up and throwing it away.

In May, it got really cold again, and Andreas came down with a cold that turned into a persistent cough. After three weeks, he still had it, so Andreas went to the doctor. The doctor listened to his breathing, and said to be on the safe side he wanted him to have a computed tomography scan. Andreas called the hospital and got an appointment for Wednesday afternoon. When Sylvie called, he made up an excuse. She laughed and accused him of having found some new hobby.

The tomography didn't take long, and it wasn't as bad as Andreas had expected. He shut his eyes, and tried to imagine he was lying on the beach in the sun, but the clattering of the machine kept bringing him back to reality.

The weather improved, and with it Andreas's mood. The doctor had prescribed some medicine, and his cough got a little better. He had almost forgotten about it by the time of his follow-up appointment. Even before he had sat down, the doctor said the results were a little worrisome. He held the picture of Andreas's lung up against the window and with his silver pen circled an area between the two wings of the lung.

"There's a chance that it's just tubercular scarring," he said.

He sat down, and twiddled with his pen. To be on the safe side, he wanted to have a biopsy done, a very minor operation sampling the tissue, which could be done on an outpatient basis.

"They make a little incision above the sternum, and insert a probe. You won't feel a thing."

"What else could it be?" asked Andreas.

The doctor told him not to worry. Andreas asked what the chances were. The doctor said it was meaningless to talk about chances.

"It's either-or. You have it or you don't."

He stood up, returned his pen to the top pocket of his white coat, and shook hands with Andreas. He said he was sorry not to have had any better news.

Andreas stood in the empty classroom. The corridor rang with the running steps and shouts of boys and girls going home. He remembered his own time at school, the last day of term before the summer holidays, the way the kids ran off in all directions once the final class was at an end. The haste with which everyone disappeared, as though they were going somewhere. His best friend hardly stopped to say good-bye as he ran off, and Andreas felt betrayed. He had dawdled, gone home slowly with the big cardboard folder containing all the drawings he had done in the year. The folder was much too big for him; he needed both arms to carry it, to prevent the drawings from slipping out. Back then, summer had been something horribly, outlandishly long, and the beginning of the new school year was unimaginably far off.

He got his things together. On his desk was a little potted plant, a yellow primrose that one of his girls had given him as a good-bye present. The pot was wrapped in tinfoil. Andreas hesitated for a moment, thought about taking the plant home with him. Then he left it. He imagined it slowly withering and dying in neglect. In the fall, other children would be sitting here, shyly eyeing the new teacher.

He stowed books and papers away in desk drawers and in his case. Then he took down the posters on the walls, the collages and placards that the kids had made over the course of the year. Germany's Constitutional System, German Cuisine, The Life of J. S. Bach. He rolled them all together, and rammed them into the wastebasket.

He walked through the empty school. He looked down at the yard through one of the tall windows. One of his pupils was sitting on a bench and kept looking anxiously toward the door. It was the boy who had been involved in the fights. Andreas wondered what he was waiting for, why he didn't go home. The boy didn't budge from where he was.

In the staff room there were still the white plastic cups for the end-of-term drinks that had been given out during the lunch break. Andreas tidied them away, along with the dirty napkins and the half-eaten rolls. He poured himself the remains of the white wine and took a sip. The wine was lukewarm and tasted sour. There was a knock, and Delphine stuck her head around the door.

"No one's here?" she asked.

"Aren't I anyone?"

"I wanted to say good-bye," said Delphine. "It's my last day today."

"Come on in," said Andreas. He found her a cup and poured her some of the wine. Delphine took a sip and shuddered.

"Disgusting," she said. But she went on drinking it just the same. When she started helping Andreas clear the table, he stopped and said the janitor would take care of it.

"Aren't you going home?" she asked.

"In a minute," said Andreas. He said he felt a little envious of her.

"Why?"

"Because you've finished here. Because you're about to walk out, and you'll never come here again."

"I'm sure I will. I'm going to visit my class. I promised them."

"Don't kid yourself."

Delphine did not speak. Presumably she knew that Andreas was right. She would go to work at a different school, teach different classes, go out with different colleagues, and wrangle with different parents.

"There's no point," said Andreas. "You can't go back."

Each time a class graduated, a couple of the pupils promised they would come back and sit in on his new class. Once, someone really had, one of his favorite pupils. He had sat right at the back on an empty chair, and had listened in for half an hour. Then he had disappeared during the break, without saying good-bye.

"I think he was just as embarrassed as I was. I felt like a con artist. The same stories, the same jokes. Only a different audience."

From his perspective her situation might indeed be enviable, said Delphine. But she would have to get used to a new place, and that wasn't easy. She had settled here, and wouldn't have minded staying.

"Do you know where you're going to go?"

"To Versailles," said Delphine. "Assuming I pass the exam. I would have preferred to go back to the South, where I come from. But for that I would have needed two hundred and seventy points. The only way I could get that many was if I were married and had a couple of kids."

Andreas asked where she lived. She said she lived in a *chambre de bonne* nearby. Before that, she'd lived in Arles, with her parents.

"My father's a policeman. I grew up in police barracks. We moved every other year."

She wanted to go back South or to the Atlantic coast. Somewhere near the sea. She loved the sea. With a name like yours, that's a surprise, said Andreas dryly. From Arles it wasn't such a long way to the sea, said Delphine. And in the summer vacation, she had always gone to the Atlantic coast with her parents. There was a police campsite near Bordeaux. It was paradise.

By the time they left the school, the boy whom Andreas had watched out of the window was no longer there.

"I've got to go this way," said Delphine, and she pointed down the street. Andreas said he'd walk her some of the way, if she didn't mind. He didn't feel like going home.

They walked along slowly side by side. Delphine talked about her class, and her qualifying exams, which she'd found difficult. Andreas asked her whether she was going to the Atlantic this summer.

"End of July," she said, "after I've found myself somewhere to live in Versailles."

They stopped in a bistro for a drink. First they stood at the bar, then they sat down in one of the little booths. Their legs touched, perhaps by chance. Andreas looked at Delphine. She was pale and her complexion was poor, but she had pretty features. Her dark hair was cut short and kept simple. She wasn't very slim, but she looked fit.

They stopped talking. Delphine looked Andreas in the eye, smiled, and lowered her gaze. She said she lived just around the corner. Her room was tiny. Andreas said the room he'd lived in for the whole of his first year in Paris hadn't been much bigger than the bed in it.

"It was in one of those cheap hotels by the station. They have wonderful names and terrible rooms. Mine was called *Hotel de la Nouvelle France*. I happened to walk past it the other day. The hotel doesn't exist anymore. The building was gutted. The sign bearing the name is still there, but only the facade is left."

He hadn't passed that way by chance. It was in a fit of nostalgia that he had gone to the neighborhood, without really knowing what he was looking for. The streets hadn't changed much to look at, but apart from the bakery and the Metro, there was no shop and no restaurant that he could recall. Over the door of his local pub there was still the sign, *Le Cordial*, but in the window there was a dusty scrap of cardboard that said *Fermé*, which was more accurate. In that first year, when Andreas came back from his nocturnal wanderings, the curtains of the bar would be drawn, and just a thin strip of light would indicate there was still anyone inside. He knocked on the glass door, and the owner pulled the curtain aside, and after looking at him suspiciously, he would unlock the door and admit Andreas. Back then, almost every night had come to an end in the *Cordial*, with crazy conversations that got ever stickier until they finally completely dried. In the morning, when Andreas took the train to work, he still felt the alcohol from the night before, and he had to make an effort not to fall asleep and miss his stop. The little room was filthy beyond description. The shelf that had once had bottles on it was empty. Tables and chairs were piled into one corner. Behind that was a photo screen that Andreas suddenly remembered one day. It was a yellowed mountain landscape, a small lake surrounded by trees, against a backdrop of snow-topped mountains. The picture must date from some previous owner. The host and most of the clientele were Algerians. Andreas wondered where Paco had got to, and his lovely wife, who had bossed her husband about like a kid.

"The hotel was wretched," said Andreas, "but I was still young. There was one shower and one toilet for twenty guests. In summer, if it was hot, you had to queue up for a shower. You had to buy coupons for warm water. If we had no money, we made do with cold showers."

"I couldn't stand that," said Delphine. "I need my own bath."

She said she would stay here until she had found a place in Versailles. But she did want to leave before the vacation.

They paid and left the bistro. Delphine went on, without either of them having said anything. Andreas loved such moments, when basically everything had been decided, but nothing had been said or done. He followed Delphine. Before, they had walked side by side, now she was in the lead, and he so close behind her that he almost touched her. She was wearing cheap clothes, jeans, a white T-shirt, and a jacket with rhinestones. Andreas had a sense that she was walking differently from before, more confidently, as though she knew what he had in mind. They didn't speak, not even when Delphine stopped in front of a building and entered a code on an electronic pad beside the door. She held it open for him, and he followed her through a courtyard and up a flight of stairs. On the fourth floor he came to a stop. He was out of breath, and coughing.

"You smoke too much," said Delphine, who was already on the next landing.

When he got to the top floor, she had disappeared. A door stood open.

The room was furnished rather basically; you could tell it had been assembled by someone who wasn't planning to use it himself. There were hardly any books on the shelf, and apart from an almost bald basil plant on the table, there were no plants. On the bed there was a sleeping bag on a bare mattress. Next to it on the floor was a huge blue IKEA plastic bag full of dirty laundry. Delphine said she would have to do her laundry tonight. Andreas went up to the little window and looked out.

"A pretty view."

"I only come here to sleep."

He turned around toward her. She had sat down on the bed and was looking at him inquiringly. He knew what she expected of him. They would kiss, make love on the stained mattress, then he would accompany her to the launderette before taking her out to dinner. Afterward they might make love a second time, while he kept an eye on his watch to be sure he didn't miss the last train. He would get dressed, and she would see him to the door, and he would turn to look at her once more on the stairs, to leave a good impression. And that would be the last either of them would ever hear of the other.

Delphine had got up and joined him in front of the window. Their shoulders brushed, and he smelled her perfume, a fresh, lemony scent. Summer, sun, and flowering meadows, he thought—it made him laugh.

"What's so funny?" asked Delphine irritably.

"I just remembered something," said Andreas, "a story I was reading. A love story."

He asked her what scent she used. She asked him whether she liked it. Yes, he said, he did. He started to laugh again. The whole situation seemed so hackneyed.

"What's the big joke?"

"You certainly confused Jean-Marc."

Delphine didn't say anything for a moment, then she asked what Jean-Marc had said.

"That you had slept with him. And that you didn't want anything to do with him."

"What a moron."

Andreas laid his hand on her shoulder. She shrugged it off.

"Don't worry," he said.

"I'm not worried."

Andreas sat down on the bed. Delphine sat down next to him. The tension was gone.

"Well?" she asked.

"He really is a moron. My best friend, the moron."

Andreas laughed, and then he started coughing. Delphine said it didn't sound good. He thanked her. Delphine said he was a strange person, and that got Andreas laughing and coughing again.

"Don't worry," he said, once he had recovered himself a little. "I won't say anything to him."

"Say what?" asked Delphine. She said Jean-Marc had been a mistake. It had been one of those evenings where you would go along with anyone at all, purely not to be alone. Did he have those, ever? She couldn't know that Jean-Marc was going to fall in love with her.

"He didn't fall in love with you," said Andreas. "It's just his vanity. If you'd followed him, called him on the phone, pestered him, he would have dropped you soon enough."

"Thanks for the compliment."

"I don't mean it like that. I know Jean-Marc. I bet he showed you photographs of his children."

"I could have murdered him," said Delphine, laughing.

They lay side by side on the mattress, and looked silently up at the ceiling. It had begun to get dark outside. Andreas felt very calm. At last, Delphine sat up. She turned and looked at Andreas.

"The launderette shuts in two hours."

"Is this one of those evenings you would go to bed with absolutely anyone?" he asked.

"No," said Delphine, and she started to undo Andreas's shirt. Her face looked quite impassive. She took off his shirt and pants, and then his shorts. Then she disappeared into the bathroom, and came back with a condom, which she carefully opened and put on him. With a few movements, she stripped off her clothes and left them bundled up on the floor. For a moment, she stood naked beside the bed, with her hands hanging down. Andreas was amazed by her pallor. He took her hand, and pulled her down on top of him.

He had meant to go to Brittany to visit Jean-Marc, who came from there, and went back every summer with his wife and kids for a few weeks. He telephoned him, and said he had to put off his visit by a few days. He gave no reason. Nor did he say anything about the biopsy to Sylvia or Nadia. He could imagine their reactions. Nadia would feel sorry for herself, first and foremost. She would be furious with him, the way people are furious with a glass when they break the glass. And Sylvie would straightaway set herself to solving the problem. She was bound to have a friend who was a lung special-

ist, and who would agree to examine Andreas, and treat
him. He left them both thinking he was off on holiday.
The only person whom Andreas told was Delphine. He
was surprised himself that he talked to her, but maybe
it was because she had no great role in his life, that he
didn't know her better than someone you meet on a trip
abroad, and then soon lose track of. Even the fact that
they had slept together didn't seem to have brought
them together. She asked him what he liked, and told
him what she liked, and told him when he was too fast
or too rough. When it was over, he really did go to the
launderette with her, and while they sat in front of the
machines waiting, he told Delphine about the biopsy.
Once again, she was cool and objective. She didn't try
to comfort him, or to play down the whole thing. She
listened to him carefully, and asked him what time he
was due at the hospital and how long it would take.
Then she said she would drive him there. He said he
could perfectly well walk, it was only fifteen minutes,
but Delphine insisted on driving him.

Five days later, she rang the bell punctually. She
had left her car in the middle of the road, and when
Andreas came out of the house, she was arguing with a
truck driver who couldn't get past. In the middle of a
sentence, she broke off, got in the car, leaned over to

the passenger seat to let Andreas in. She gestured at the truck driver, and drove off.

The hospital was right behind the Gare du Nord. Andreas walked right past it every day on his way to work, and had never noticed it was there. Delphine drew up outside the main entrance, and kissed him on the mouth.

"Good luck," she said. She said she wouldn't be far away. He was to call her when he was finished.

"I've no idea how long it'll be," said Andreas.

"Doesn't matter. I've got something to read."

The operation itself didn't take long, but afterward Andreas had to go and lie down for a couple of hours, even though he'd only been given a local anesthetic. When they told him he could go, he called Delphine. She said she'd be there in fifteen minutes. He was to wait for her at the entrance. He went out into the big hospital forecourt, ringed by three-story buildings of light-colored sandstone. The complex put him in mind of a barracks or prison. In the middle of the yard was a piece of lawn surrounded by a low hedge, at the far end of it was a tower with a clock. It was half past four. The yard was deserted, except for the occasional doctor or nurse crossing it with quick steps. It was astonishingly quiet, with no sense of the bustling city beyond.

Andreas tried to imagine what it would be like to have to spend weeks or months here, to have a bed behind one of the windows, and lie there weakened after an operation or a course of therapy. He would barely be able to take the few steps to the window, or out into the corridor. He was too weak to wish to be anywhere other than in bed, back in the semi-stupor in which he spent his nights and days. Then, in the middle of the night once, he found himself wide awake. He listened. It was raining outside, and the noise of the rain mingled with the sounds of his neighbor breathing. He got up and left the ward. He walked through darkened corridors and down wide staircases to the exit. He snuck past the porter, walked through the city, barefoot and in pajamas. Catch cold, he was thinking, catch my death of cold. Those strange sentences. A patrol car followed him for a while, but he slipped away through a pedestrian street.

Andreas emerged onto the street. A couple of tourists were hurriedly lugging big plastic suitcases across the road to the station. For a moment he thought of catching the next train, never mind where to, anywhere they wouldn't be able to find him. He failed to spot Delphine, who was parked only a few yards away. She had to wind down the window and call his name.

Delphine moved freely about the apartment, as if she had been there many times before. She made tea for Andreas. She found everything right away, the teabags, the teapot, the matches to light the gas.

Andreas, wearing pajamas, was lying down on the sofa. He felt freezing, though it wasn't cold. Delphine brought him a blanket from the bedroom, and sat down in a chair opposite him. He smiled, and she furrowed her brow.

"What are you, my lover or my nurse?"

"I'm used to it," she said. "My mother was often sick."

Andreas was surprised his situation didn't feel more awkward to him. When he'd been ill before, he would crawl into a corner, and refuse any offers of help or visits. Now, though, he was glad Delphine was with him, looking after him and talking to him.

"Was it very bad?"

"It didn't hurt, and it doesn't hurt now. But the idea of them cutting you open and shoving something inside you, that's terrible."

He said he didn't want to talk about it now. He wanted to rest. Delphine asked him whether he would like her to read aloud to him. She went over to the bookshelf, and browsed through the titles.

"Jack London," she said, "wasn't he that gold miner? What are you in the mood for? *Understanding Germany? Switzerland from the Air, The Judge and His Hangman? A Short Grammar of the German Language,* Bertolt Brecht?"

She groaned.

"Can you read German?"

Delphine said she had taken it at school, but forgotten most of it. Andreas pointed her to the little book on the coffee table. That was fairly simple, he said, school level. Delphine worked out the title.

"*Love Without Frontiers,*" she said. "And you give that kind of thing to your kids?"

"No," said Andreas, and shut his eyes. Delphine cleared her throat and began to read.

It was on a warm spring day that I saw Angélique for the first time. I knew right away that she wasn't from here. She wore different clothes from the local girls. The girls here all go around in jeans. They ride bikes, and they talk as loudly as the boys. Angélique was wearing a skirt. She was walking through the village. She was carrying a shopping basket, and she was looking around curiously.

Delphine read softly and slowly. Sometimes she got her stresses so wrong that Andreas had to concentrate hard to follow the text. After a while he gave up the effort, and just followed the sound of her voice.

He tried to picture Fabienne walking in the village, but he couldn't do it. He could barely remember her face. He saw Sylvie and Nadia and the teacher with the big breasts, and, when he briefly opened his eyes, Delphine, leaning over the book and slowly and with difficulty forming German sentences that she could probably not understand more than half of. He remembered the first lessons in the German book, the language tapes, the friendly detached voice speaking nonsensical sentences: *The grass is green. The sky is blue. The pine is tall.* And then the expectant silence that made the sentences into questions. Was the grass really green? Was the sky blue? And then the voice a second time, repeating the sentence. The grass was green, and the world was the way it had always been.

Andreas remembered meeting Fabienne for the first time. It was at a twentieth birthday party for Manuel's sister Beatrice, with whom he went out later. At the time he barely knew Beatrice. He had met her a couple of times while doing homework with Manuel. Presumably she had invited him because of her brother, who didn't have many friends. At the time, Fabienne was newly arrived in the village. He couldn't remember where Beatrice knew her from.

The party was in a cottage in the woods. The woods were bordered on one side by industrial terrain and a gravel pit, but the hut was on the other, by the river. When Andreas arrived, there was a big fire already going. Young men and women stood around talking. He propped his bike against a tree, and watched as they went around getting things ready. Most of the guests he knew vaguely by sight. A couple of young men came out of the forest with huge bundles of wood, which they dropped on the ground beside the fire. Beatrice was peeling clingwrap off bowls of salad, and Manuel was pricking sausages. Fabienne caught Andreas's eye right away. She never left Beatrice's side.

After they had eaten, Beatrice unpacked the presents, and asked who each one was from, and thanked the people without looking at them properly. Andreas's present was a book by Albert Camus that he had only recently read himself. The two young men who had brought the wood were now burning cardboard plates and napkins on the fire. Andreas watched as the laminated finish on the plates bubbled up before the plates suddenly caught fire and were consumed with a greenish flame in a matter of seconds.

A birthday cake was produced, and Beatrice and Fabienne pumped coffee from a giant thermos flask.

One of the young men had brought a guitar, and Christian songs were sung that Andreas didn't know.

> *Time hurries by, the hours fly,*
> *and no one stops them.*
> *Your years too are rushing by*
> *like a bird in flight.*

Fabienne looked ravishing in the firelight. When their eyes met, she smiled. She seemed not to know the songs either.

Someone began telling jokes. Then Beatrice suggested playing hide and seek. Everyone paired off, and because most of the guests knew each other from the Christian youth group, and a few of them were couples already, at the end only Fabienne and Andreas were left over. Beatrice explained the rules, and told people not to go too far. She and her friend stayed by the fire, and started counting down.

The wood was bright, the moon was almost full, but it was hard keeping your bearings. The noise and the laughter of the others could be heard from all sides, as they stumbled over the uneven forest floor. Andreas followed a narrow path. Fabienne followed him at a distance. They had yet to exchange a word. After about fifty yards they left the path and came to a little hollow.

"What about here," whispered Andreas. He crouched down and looked back in the direction of the hut, where the light of the fire, now almost burned down, shone weakly. Then he heard Beatrice call: "Ready or not, here we come!"

Fabienne was leaning against a tree, as though she didn't care whether she was found or not. They waited. Shouts and laughter were heard in the forest. The first couple were found, and joined in the search. They seemed to be walking along the edge of the forest, their voices getting louder and then quieter. The fire had flared up once more, and then collapsed into itself. Now you couldn't make it out anymore.

"They'll never find us in the dark," said Fabienne. It was the first sentence that Andreas heard from her mouth. She spoke French. He asked her where she was from. Paris, she said, her parents lived on the outskirts of Paris.

After some time, Andreas got up, and they crept back to the hut. Only Manuel was there, poking the embers with a branch. The others had gone to the gravel pit, he said. Fabienne and Andreas sat down, and Manuel started asking Fabienne questions. And in the end, they arranged to go swimming on Sunday.

When Andreas awoke, it was still dark. Delphine was still sitting in her chair, her legs stretched out on the coffee table, asleep. The book was in her lap.

Andreas wondered what she was doing here. He was almost twice her age, and had no idea what there was for her in making tea for a sick man and reading him children's stories. They barely knew each other.

He undid the top buttons of his pajama jacket, and prodded the bandage over the wound. It didn't hurt, but the thought of the incision beneath the bandage made him feel nauseous. He got up to go to the bathroom. When he returned, Delphine was up. He asked her if she didn't have to go. She said she had nothing planned.

"If you like, I'll stay the night with you."

"I'm not up to much, I'm afraid."

Delphine told him not to be stupid, sex wasn't everything. She asked him if he was hungry. He shook his head.

"You must eat."

She went into the kitchen. Andreas heard her open and shut the fridge. She called over to say she would go out and buy a couple of things, was there a store nearby that was still open. Andreas said there was a greengrocer on the corner who stayed open till midnight. She said she'd be back right away. He wanted to give her some money, but by the time he was in the hall, she was already gone. Andreas had never lived together with a woman. It was a strange feeling, having someone moving around in his apartment, and going shopping and cooking for him.

He went back to the sitting room, and stopped in front of the mantel. His eye fell on a little framed photograph there. His father had taken it before Andreas had gone to Paris. It was one of the few things Andreas had wanted to keep when his father died. He picked up the picture and looked at it, and then at himself in the mirror over the mantel. He was startled by how little he had changed. His features had gotten a little harder, but the basic expression was still the same, an expression of friendly indifference.

Andreas studied the inscrutable expression, just as strange to him now as it was at the time it was taken. When pictures were put up in the staff room from a party or a graduation, he often couldn't recognize himself in them, and when he looked at them he couldn't remember how he had felt when they were taken. He remembered his father taking that picture. They had gone out into the garden together. His father had got Andreas to stand in the shade under the sumac, and then sheepishly clicked the release a couple of times. It was the hopeless wish to capture his son. Presumably that had occurred to Andreas too, because he had a smile on his lips, half sympathetic, half-mocking. Only much later did it dawn on him how brave and affectionate it had been on the part of his father.

Not many days later, Andreas had left. He still remembered the silent leave-taking from his father. It was a Saturday, and the local train was packed with people going to the next village, or to the city, to go to the cinema or the theater. Andreas felt he stood out, with his big suitcase and his far-off destination. When the train pulled away, his father waved. His lips moved, perhaps to say something. Andreas briefly raised his hand. He was embarrassed. Only later had he understood that he would never be able to go back to the village. A few months later, when he went home for a visit during the vacation, everything felt different. After that, his visits were rarer and rarer, and finally they stopped altogether.

Andreas put the photograph back on the mantelpiece. He had never had many pictures of his family.

The few that he had been given lay in a drawer some-where. He wondered what had possessed him to put this one out—a picture of himself.

It was ten o'clock. Delphine was in the kitchen, chop-ping vegetables. Andreas watched her. She said he could go and lie down, it would be at least another quarter of an hour till the soup was ready.

"Why are you doing this?"

"Doing what?"

"You could be going to the cinema or meeting friends or what do I know."

"It's second nature. If a friend is ill . . . Anyway, I went to the cinema yesterday."

"I can make soup for myself," said Andreas. "Any-way, we're not friends. We hardly know each other."

Delphine put down the knife and looked at him in astonishment. She said if he was bothered by her being there, he just had to tell her. Andreas apologized. He said he hadn't meant it in a bad way.

After supper, he said he would go to bed, the op-eration had taken more out of him than he had first thought. Delphine carried the dirty dishes out. He heard her washing up, and putting the plates away.

She had her toiletry bag with her, but no nightie. She said she hadn't been sure what she intended to happen, and so she had struck a sort of deal with herself. Andreas lent her a T-shirt, and she went to the bathroom. He heard her showering, then she came out and lay down next to him on the bed. She leaned across him, kissed him on the mouth and said good night.

"Come here," he said, "I'm not that sick."

She said he ought to be careful. She pulled the T-shirt over her head, and scooted over to him. Her body was soft and warm and sluggish. I don't love her, thought Andreas, I don't even want her really. Delphine sat on him, and slowly began to move. They were both very calm and quiet. Once, Andreas almost fell asleep, he dropped into a dream for a moment, and then he opened his eyes and saw Delphine, still sitting astride him and moving in a very concentrated way, as if in a slow dance.

"You almost fell asleep," she said with a smile.

"Don't stop," he said.

The next day Delphine went to Versailles to look at a few apartments. In the early afternoon she was back. She was carrying a sports bag with a few clothes.

"Are you planning on moving in?"

"Would you mind?"

"Well, if it's just for a few days."

Delphine said he needn't worry. She was going away on vacation at the end of the month anyway.

"The end of the month!" said Andreas, with mock-horror. "And what do I do then?"

"Come and visit me if you want. I've got my own tent. And my parents are nice people." She grinned and said her parents were about his age.

He said he had intended to go to Brittany to stay with Jean-Marc.

"Don't worry," said Delphine, but then she didn't say anything else.

Andreas was less tired than he'd been the day before. They took the Metro down to the Seine, and walked along the banks. The sun was shining, and there were a lot of people out enjoying themselves, with dogs and bicycles and rollerblades.

"Sometimes I think Paris is one gigantic stage set," said Andreas.

"Have you ever tried that?" asked Delphine.

"Rollerblading? I'm too old for that. I can remember a time when skates had four wheels, like cars."

"Did cars even exist back then? Have you got a thing about being old?"

Andreas asked her how old she was.

"When you were born, I was in the middle of puberty," he said.

"So?"

He didn't often think about his age, said Andreas. He had never had the feeling of being old; he thought of himself as somehow ageless. Perhaps his cough was getting to him a little bit.

On his fortieth birthday he had had a little party, largely because Jean-Marc and Marthe had forced him to. But he had never understood the fuss about those so-called round-numbered birthdays. The only thing that had bothered him then was that he wasn't too sure whom to ask. He got on all right with most of his colleagues, but he would never have described them as friends, and he certainly didn't feel like celebrating his birthday with them. He couldn't invite Sylvie and Nadia together, and various other ex-girlfriends he was still in touch with weren't really guest material either. In the end, it was a small gathering, a dinner party, not a party. And Jean-Marc and Marthe needed all their persuasive powers to make Andreas go out dancing with them afterward.

"Do you have a bad feeling about the result?" asked Delphine.

They had sat down on a bench, and watched people strolling by.

"I don't know," said Andreas. "I try not to think about it."

"Then let's go and do something. Let's see a movie."

He didn't feel like it, he said. He just wanted to sit here a bit and look at the people and enjoy the sunshine, like cats, or like old people. "Did you notice how many old men stand around in the city, on corners or in front of building sites? Always standing around, with frightened-looking expressions on their faces, watching their time go by."

They walked on. Later they ate in a restaurant near the Tour Montparnasse. Delphine said she had never been up the tower. Did he feel like going up with her? Another time perhaps, said Andreas, he was tired after their walk.

"Did you know there was a rue de Départ here, and a rue d'Arrivée?"

"Of course," said Delphine, "and in between is the Place Bienvenue."

"That I didn't know."

"And I've only been living here for a year," Delphine said proudly.

Three days later, Andreas got a call from his doctor's office. The assistant said the hospital had sent the results, and asked him to drop by. Andreas asked whether the results were positive. The assistant said that, even if she knew, she wasn't allowed to tell him. He asked if he might come over right away. In half an hour, she replied. Delphine was off in Versailles again, looking at more apartments. He left her a note, saying he had gone out and would be back soon.

On the way to the doctor's, he told himself a hundred times that the result, whatever it was, didn't change his condition, that it was already decided whether he was healthy or sick. Even though he walked slowly, he started to sweat, and felt a little nauseous. He could hardly make it up the stairs.

The assistant told him he would have to be patient a little longer, and asked him to take a seat in the waiting room. He thought she was looking at him rather pityingly. The waiting room was bare. There were chairs along the walls, a table in the middle of the room, with a few tattered magazines on it. A woman was sitting on one of the chairs. She had a child on her lap whose face was half-covered with a purple birthmark. The child was whimpering. The woman spoke to it quietly, and promised it chocolate if it was quiet. Andreas had taken a magazine off the table, a Catholic parents' magazine. He read an article on the advantages of breast-feeding, but without being able to concentrate on it. The assistant came out and called a name. The woman got up and took her child by the hand. It started to scream, and clung on to the chair with its other hand.

"Always the same fuss," said the woman, with an apologetic look in Andreas's direction.

The assistant unclasped the child's hand, finger by finger, and together the two women dragged the screaming child out onto the corridor. Andreas stared at the wall, which had a faded Chagall poster on it, from an exhibition he had actually been to many years ago. At the time, he had liked those pictures; now he had no use for them anymore. He took a couple of deep breaths, then he got up and left the room.

The assistant was standing with her back to him in the doorway of the surgery. The mother and child were not to be seen, though the shrill screams of the child were clearly audible. Andreas crept to the exit. He left the office and shut the door after him.

He stopped for a moment at the top of the stairs. Then he heard someone coming up the stairs, and he started to panic. He felt as though no one must see him here. He climbed up a flight of stairs and waited until he heard the door open and shut downstairs.

He left the building, and walked briskly down the street. He asked himself how many people knew about his condition. It alarmed him that there was a file with his name on it, and that there were photographs of his insides, and somewhere some tissue samples that had been taken from him. Someone had made a diagnosis and come to certain decisions about him, someone he didn't even know. He had no choice. The machinery was in motion. We'll take a tissue sample, the doctor had said. It wasn't a question, it wasn't even a command. You didn't bother issuing commands to a victim, you just got on with it. The doctor who had performed the little operation had shaken hands with him and introduced herself. He couldn't remember her name. The nurse and the anesthetist didn't have names, just their functions. They were as anonymous for him as he was to them.

Andreas walked on and on in a straight line. He wasn't going anywhere, he just wanted to get out of the neighborhood. He was running away from the disease that was his life, his work, his apartment, the people he called friends or lovers. Here on the street no one recognized him, he was just a pedestrian like a thousand others, who passed him or whom he passed. Here he had no past and no future, only a fleeting present. He had to keep walking on, he mustn't stop, mustn't linger, then nothing could happen to him.

The sky was overcast, but it was warm. Andreas was sweating. His body felt strange to him, unresponsive. It moved somehow independently of him. Onward, ever onward. He reached the Seine, and followed it west. He saw the Eiffel Tower loom up, and left it behind. He was on the narrow Swan's Island, approaching the little Statue of Liberty, the model for that other one that the French gave the Americans to celebrate their independence. He had often come here during his early time in Paris. When he was sad and alone. After Fabienne had left for Switzerland, and later, when a woman had finished with him, he had come here, and stood under weeping willows and watched the freighters, and surveyed the ugly office blocks on the south bank. It was one of the few parts of Paris that wasn't beautiful, one of the few places that didn't have that silver patina, the patina he adored when he was feeling good, but that he couldn't stand at times like this.

Andreas imagined how he would tell Delphine about his illness, or Nadia and Sylvie and Jean-Marc.

Isn't it hot today. How was your vacation? Oh, by the way, I've got cancer. Everyone would get to hear about it, his colleagues, the school administration, the pupils. Maybe they would have to operate on him and give him radiation treatment. He would have a course of chemotherapy. He pictured himself in the school with no hair or a silly cap. Everyone staring at him, knowing the situation, pitying him. They would presume to discuss him and his "case," his tragic case. They whispered behind his back. When they talked to him face to face, they would pretend nothing was different. But he would be a patient in everything he said and did.

He lit a cigarette, but it didn't taste good, and he dropped it disgustedly in the river.

They would start to avoid him. He remembered a colleague from a few years back, a French teacher, who had a brain tumor. He had gone out of the man's way himself. He hadn't even turned up for the little drinks party the colleague had given for his leaving. He left some pathetic excuse. When they had a collection a few months later, for flowers, he put in far too much. Now he would be the one to whose health they would drink, whose grave flowers they would collect.

There had to be another way. There was always another way. Perhaps the patch really was just the scarring from some old tuberculosis, or it was a benign tumor. Even if the results were bad, nothing was certain. The lab could have made a mistake. The samples could have gotten mixed up with someone else's. It was a tiny chance, but there it was. Andreas didn't want to know. They couldn't force him to know. As long as he didn't know anything, nothing could happen to him. He had to get away from here. He had to begin a new life. That, he thought, is my only chance.

His decision spurred him on. It was as though he had got back control over his own life, as though, maybe for the first time since going to Paris, he had his life in his hands again. He would heal himself of his past life, which hadn't been one. From now on, he would determine things himself. He would make his own decisions, and leave them all, one after another, and, last of all, himself. He called Nadia, but she wasn't home. Sylvie was in a rush, as always. He asked if she had any time tomorrow. "But tomorrow is Saturday," she said, "you know, family day."

"Just very quickly," said Andreas. "I've got something I want to say to you."

Sylvie laughed. They agreed to meet tomorrow afternoon, somewhere near her apartment. Half an hour, she said, not a second more.

In the apartment, Delphine was waiting for him. She had been worried. She asked what had kept him so long. Andreas was irritated by her question and the way Delphine had taken over and claimed he owed her an explanation. He looked at her in silence.

"What's the matter?"

"I got my results," he said. He reflected for a moment, and then he smiled. "Everything's fine—couldn't be better."

"Really?" asked Delphine, as though she couldn't believe it. Then she flung herself at him. She kissed him on the mouth a couple of times, and said now they had to celebrate. He felt suspicious of her joy, looked for signs of disappointment in her eyes. Most people—and here he didn't exclude himself—preferred the misfortune of others to ordinary dull day-to-day life. But Delphine seemed to be genuinely happy. She wouldn't stop hugging him, and rubbing his chest with the flat of her hand, as though giving him some kind of first-aid.

Andreas took her to the *Vieux Moulin*, a restaurant that was only a short distance from his house, though he didn't often go there. The food was expensive, and the staff were moody, because the place was usually half-empty. They ate oysters and some main course the waiter recommended, and they shared a bottle of wine.

"I thought you were a vegetarian," Delphine said.

Andreas replied that he wasn't a vegetarian, he just didn't eat meat all that often. But now he felt like it.

"I'm a new man," he said, and rolled his shoulders. "I'm going to start all over again."

"And do everything differently," laughed Delphine.

"And do everything differently," said Andreas.

"Right. And now we're going dancing," said Delphine.

Andreas protested, but it was no use.

It was very loud in the discotheque. They bought drinks at the bar, and watched the dancers for a while. Then Delphine took Andreas by the hand and led him out onto the dance floor. She went on ahead, dodging through the mass of people. She walked on light feet, like a cat, or a model, he thought. Andreas stared at her bottom, then she spun around, pushed his hand aside, and drew him against her. She beamed, kissed him on the mouth, laid her other hand on his shoulder. She seemed to be unaware of the rhythm of the music, until Andreas took over. When that happened, Delphine laughed, a silent laugh that the music drowned out. Her head went right back, and Andreas thought either she's drunk or she's happy, it doesn't matter, comes to the same thing. He too was drunk with the wine and the loud music and the flashing lights. And perhaps he was happy as well, or just excited, he couldn't tell. He wasn't sick, for a moment he almost believed it himself. He turned his head this way and that while he danced, he looked at other women, but it was only Delphine he wanted to dance with, who held his face in her hands to make him look at her, and then let him go again. A strobe light cut the movements of the dancers into individual stills, and then the colored lights came back on, and everything gleamed in red, and blue, and red again. Delphine spun around Andreas's hand, lost the beat, and hugged him clumsily, while the other couples jigged up and down around them.

The music seemed to have gotten quieter, Andreas had the sensation of floating, he was moving in slow motion. He held Delphine, and she gripped him, then he picked up the beat and took Delphine with him. The music was back again, and louder than before. The DJ sang something, and the dancers sang along, no one seemed to have understood the words, they were all just mimicking the sounds, as though they were in a foreign language that was all vowels, meaningless words, a pounding rhythm, a song that imperceptibly segued into another, and then another.

Delphine leaned up to Andreas and shouted in his ear that she wanted to sleep with him, right now.

"Here?" Andreas yelled back. Delphine didn't understand him, so he yelled "Here?" again.

She punched him playfully on the shoulder, and dragged him off the dance floor.

Andreas didn't turn the lights on in the apartment. He opened all the windows. There was a light in the yard, and its orange glow suffused everything in the apartment. Delphine had followed Andreas into the bedroom, and he started undressing her. When she was naked, he took off the ring she wore on one finger, and her little earrings as well. She laughed and asked him what he was doing. He didn't answer. While they made love, he told her to look at him. At first she wouldn't and turned her head away, but then she did, and it seemed to excite her as it excited him. Her pupils were dilated in the dim light, and her eyes looked as though they were made of glass.

Andreas and Delphine lay side by side, sweating. She had her palm on his thigh, and was stroking it mechanically. She asked him what he was thinking.

"I want you to leave," he said.

"Leave where?"

"Go home."

"Now?"

"Yes," said Andreas. "Don't be upset, just I'd prefer to be on my own."

He had thought Delphine would resist. But instead she got up without a word, went in the bathroom and showered. She came back, and got together her clothes and her jewelry in the dark. Andreas felt like making love to her again, and for an instant he regretted having sent her away. He got up and embraced her from behind. She shook him away.

"Can you understand how I might feel used?"

"I might as well say I've been used by you."

She laughed, a cackling sort of laugh, bewildered, not malicious.

"If you want to feel like a victim," said Andreas, "fine by me. Just go."

Delphine turned the light on and furiously got dressed. She stuffed her things in the sports bag.

When she was gone, Andreas showered and got dressed. Even though he'd drunk a lot of wine, he felt clear-headed. He felt like a secret agent, carrying out a plan that no one besides him knew. He looked at the clock. It was a little after midnight. He thought of giving Nadia a call, but then he had another idea.

He walked quickly, and was rather out of breath as he stood outside Nadia's house, twenty minutes later. He rang the bell. It took a long time until he heard her voice on the intercom. She sounded tired.

"Can I come up?" he asked.

"Are you mad? It's . . . Do you know what time it is?"

"Half past midnight," said Andreas. "I wanted to say good-bye."

"I thought you were already on vacation."

"I'm not going anywhere. I'm leaving Paris."

There was a click on the intercom. The lock buzzed.

The front door of the apartment was open. Just coming, called Nadia from the bathroom. Andreas hadn't often been here. He went into the kitchen. The sink was full of dirty dishes, on the table was an empty wine bottle and a couple of glasses. In the fridge, Andreas found an almost empty bottle of champagne, with a silver spoon in its neck. He looked around for a clean glass. He didn't find one, and finally just tipped the end of the bottle into a teacup. When he threw the bottle in the trash, he saw some Chinese takeout containers on top. In a little cardboard box that had a few dried scraps of rice in it lay a used condom.

The living room was a mess as well. Books, magazines, and clothes were scattered on the floor. On the sofa was a brimming ashtray that fell on the ground when Andreas sat down. He stood up again, and went into the corridor.

After a while, Nadia came out of the bathroom. She was wearing her nightdress with a loose robe thrown over it. She had put on makeup and done her hair.

"An unexpected visitor," she said and smiled, a mixture of uncertain and offended. She seemed not yet to have made up her mind how she was going to respond to him.

"I should have called," said Andreas. "I didn't know it was someone else's turn today."

"I had a visitor. An old girlfriend."

Andreas said he hadn't come to check up on her. He didn't care who she slept with. He had spent the evening with someone else too. Nadia said she wasn't interested. She said she'd had enough of him. He used her like a prostitute. She didn't want to see him anymore.

"I came to say good-bye to you," said Andreas.

Nadia told him not to act so sensitive. It was nothing to do with her, said Andreas, he was leaving Paris. Nadia sighed and said, if he must know, her ex-husband had been around.

"Your horrible ex," said Andreas. "You've been seeing him the whole time, haven't you?"

That was none of his business, said Nadia. Why shouldn't she, anyway. They were both free to do as they pleased. She and her husband got along better now than before their separation.

"But who will you go to to complain about him when I'm gone?" asked Andreas. "Oh, you'll find someone soon enough. Or I can put you onto someone, a friend of mine. Do you want his number?"

"Bastard," said Nadia icily.

"I'll miss you," said Andreas. "I always used to feel so alone when I was with you."

"You're always alone, no matter who's with you," said Nadia.

The next day Andreas got up early. He had left the windows open all night, and the apartment felt chilly. He had a violent coughing fit. He felt a little ashamed of the way he had behaved with Nadia and Delphine. He was surprised at the malevolence there had been in him. But what was done was done. They would get over it. At least they wouldn't miss him.

After breakfast, he wrote a letter to the school administration, handing in his notice. He wasn't sure how long the notice period was, but he didn't care. If I'm not there anymore, I'm not there, he thought. Then he went to the realtor who had sold him the apartment ten years before. The realtor remembered the apartment, or claimed to. He said Andreas probably stood to get twice what he had paid then, even though it was tricky selling an apartment in the middle of summer. Andreas said the price was not so important, the main thing was getting the apartment off his hands. He was going to Brittany for a few days. The realtor gave him a form to fill out, and promised to do his best. Andreas gave him a key.

At noon, he called Sylvie at home. Her husband picked up. Andreas asked him to tell his wife he couldn't make this afternoon. In fact, he wouldn't see her again, ever.

"Who is this?" asked Sylvie's husband.

"Well, put it this way, I'm not her hairdresser," said Andreas, and hung up.

In the afternoon, his mobile rang. When he saw Sylvie's number flash up, he decided not to answer. She left him a message saying, had he taken leave of his senses? He knew he couldn't call her at home. It had taken her half an hour to calm her husband. And what did he mean, he couldn't see her again? Her voice sounded equally amused and annoyed. What a great woman, thought Andreas, she won't have any trouble finding someone for her afternoons.

The journey to Brittany was ghastly. Every last seat was taken on the train. There weren't any smoking compartments, and only in Rennes did they stop long enough for him to get out and smoke a cigarette. The platform was full of people greedily smoking, listening nervously for loudspeaker announcements, and looking up at the clock.

Andreas arrived in Brest a little before half past nine at night. It was still light. No sooner had he got out than he lit a cigarette. Jean-Marc was waiting for him at the end of the platform. They shook hands.

"Finish your cigarette," said Jean-Marc. "Are you hungry? We've eaten already. We had to put the children to bed."

Andreas said he had eaten a sandwich on the train. Jean-Marc offered to carry his bag. Andreas declined. He wasn't that ill, he said.

"Are you ill?"

"Just an irritating cough. It's nothing really."

The drive to Lanveoc took an hour. It was a winding road, and Andreas had to concentrate so that he didn't feel sick.

"Is the sea warm?" he asked.

"Warm enough," said Jean-Marc. "We've been swimming every day we've been here. Only Marthe doesn't go in the water. For her, it has to be twenty-five degrees."

Andreas thought of Marthe as a typical Parisian. She was interested in culture, read a lot, and went to exhibitions and classical concerts. She was slim and seemed taller than she was. She wore elegant but practical clothes, and had dyed her hair, which she wore in a bob, for as long as he'd known her. He often asked himself what she saw in Jean-Marc. It was hardly possible for two people to be more different. In spite of that, they seemed to get along pretty well. Sometimes Andreas envied them their life, which seemed to be so straightforward. When Jean-Marc talked about the children, clamoring for new running shoes or clothes like the

clothes their friends had. When he planned his vacation
and dragged back piles of brochures for holiday cottages
that all looked the same. Was there money for a new car?
Maybe next year. Or they might do it on installments.
He comparison shopped for weeks, poring over technical data and prices. Once, Jean-Marc had entered a
marathon. The preparations for that took up six months.
He managed to finish in the first third, and told everyone about it with such childish pride that no one could
be offended. Andreas pictured Jean-Marc and Marthe
sitting at home in their living room, calculating, planning their vacation, watching TV. How easily they
laughed, as they told each other the most ordinary
things. Even when they complained, they did it laugh-
ingly, as if it was all a joke.

"How did you two meet?" he asked.

"I was in the same soccer team as her brother. I
knew her already when she was a little girl. But it only
really started when we met again at his wedding, years
later."

He seemed to want to say something more, but then
he didn't. His good humor had something artificial about
it, and even though he was tanned, he seemed tired.

The house was on the edge of the village, on the
road in. It had belonged to Jean-Marc's parents. They

had moved into an old people's home some years ago, and since that time he and his siblings had used the house as a holiday home. Marthe was sitting in the living room, watching a political debate on TV. She greeted Andreas casually, without getting up. She too looked tired. Jean-Marc showed Andreas up to his room.

"Well, you know where everything is," he said. "Come down whenever you're ready. I've opened a bottle of wine. It's good stuff."

Andreas unpacked his bag and washed his face and hands in the bathroom. He tried to be quiet, so that he didn't wake the children. As he came down the stairs, he heard loud voices from the kitchen. The door was ajar. He knocked and walked in. Jean-Marc was sitting at the table, and Marthe was leaning against the sink. Neither spoke, but they had clearly been arguing.

"Everything all right?" asked Jean-Marc, getting up. He put his arm around Andreas. "I'm glad you're here."

He got a glass out of the cupboard, filled it, and handed it to Andreas.

"Shall we sit outside?"

"It's too cold," said Marthe.

"Then put something on," said Jean-Marc irritably. "I'm sure Andreas will want to smoke."

Marthe walked to the door. As she passed Andreas, she briefly put her hand on his arm, and asked him how long he planned on staying. Andreas said he didn't know. As long as they could stand to have him.

Marthe and Jean-Marc sat shoulder to shoulder in a rusty love seat. Andreas refilled their glasses. It was very quiet. There was only the croaking of frogs to be heard, and the occasional car that whined past.

"They drive like madmen here," said Marthe. "Last year someone killed himself, just a couple of hundred yards away."

"On purpose?"

Jean-Marc shook his head. "No, a drunk," he said. "It was the middle of the night. He didn't take the corner and went head-on into a tree. The tree was OK."

"Jean-Marc's little brother was here when it happened. Pascal, you've met him. He repaints cars."

"He's got his own business now," said Jean-Marc, and pushed off with both feet. The love seat swung back and forth a few times, creaking. Marthe said she was glad Andreas was here. Jean-Marc was out all day with the kids, and she got bored all by herself in the house.

"They're just like him. Nothing but sports. The idea that they might sit down and read a book . . ."

"That's not true."

"When was the last time you were at an art exhibition? Or the theater?"

Jean-Marc pretended to think about it.

"That was the time with that . . . what's her name? The blond," he said at last.

"A German artist," said Marthe. "That was six months ago."

"She paints naked men," said Jean-Marc. "Of course Marthe thinks it's wonderful. She pretends she's interested in art. All she wants to see is cock."

Marthe rolled her eyes and said, God knew, there had been enough naked women in the history of painting. Why not men for a change. Of course, there was a tremendous fuss over it. But there were just beautiful paintings. Anyway, the woman painted clothed men too. And landscapes. She asked if Andreas knew Robert Mapplethorpe. He nodded.

"You should have seen Jean-Marc at the exhibition," said Marthe. "He was going crazy."

"They're not really that big," said Jean-Marc. "If you use a wide-angle lens, the foreground always looks bigger. It's a distortion."

Marthe laughed maliciously. She said it was a pity she didn't have a wide-angle lens at her disposal. There was obviously something going on between them. Andreas made some remark about Mapplethorpe's flower photographs, and Jean-Marc started swinging again. They talked about one of their colleagues, a French teacher, who had got divorced recently.

"Andreas did the right thing," said Jean-Marc. "He never married."

"Are you with someone at the moment?"

"You can't ask him that."

"Delphine," said Andreas. "Do you know her? She was a trainee at the school this past year."

Marthe and Jean-Marc glanced at each other and said nothing. Andreas wondered whether Marthe knew anything about Jean-Marc's infidelity with Delphine, and whether that was what they'd been quarreling about. In the end, Jean-Marc sat up straight. He looked furiously at Andreas.

"Obviously, she's sleeping her way round the entire staff room," he said.

Marthe laughed aloud, and rather artificially. Jean-Marc stood up and went inside. He walked slowly, as though he was very tired.

"More wine?" asked Andreas.

Marthe leaned forward and held out her glass. He poured. He sensed there was something she wanted to say, and he waited for her. She drank.

"Cold," she said, and she laughed again. She said she and Jean-Marc had a kind of tacit agreement.

"What do you mean?"

"He can do whatever he likes. As long as I don't get to hear about it. And as long as he doesn't fall in love."

"What about you?"

"Same with me, naturally."

She said that of course the agreement had failed. Jean-Marc had fallen in love with Delphine. He had admitted it to her last night. They hadn't slept all night, and talked about separating. The fact that Andreas was now going out with Delphine of course changed everything. She stopped to think.

"Or then again, maybe not," she said.

They drank their wine in silence. After a time, Marthe said she sometimes dreamed of going to bed with another man.

"We've been married for fifteen years. We're old hands. But sometimes you find yourself longing for another pair of eyes, a different hand on your neck."

She spoke very softly. Andreas had sat down next to her on the swing. He put his arm around her. She drew up her knees, and leaned against him. She said again she was glad he was there. Andreas began to stroke Marthe's hair. She didn't seem to object, and he caressed her ear, her cheek, her neck. When he began to nuzzle her neck, she stood up, and looked at him with amusement.

"Come on, you've already taken Delphine away from him," she said.

"I'm not thinking about Jean-Marc," said Andreas. He didn't like the way his voice sounded. He felt like a caricature of a seducer. He was a little shocked himself, that he was prepared to give up a male friendship that had lasted many years, in order to sleep with the man's wife. But that was the way of it.

Marthe ran her hand through his hair as one might do to a little boy, and said she had enough trouble as it was. He got up and followed her into the house. Jean-Marc was sitting in the kitchen. He had his elbows on the table, and was staring into space. He looked like Andreas's idea of a Breton farmer. Marthe and Andreas passed him in silence, and walked upstairs.

"Good night," said Marthe, and kissed Andreas on the mouth.

He took her around the waist again, but she shook him off.

"No," she said. "Maybe another time. When everything's over."

"You'll get through it OK," said Andreas.

"I don't think so," said Marthe.

When Andreas came down in the morning, Jean-Marc wasn't up yet. The children were at the beach, Marthe said. Did he want coffee?

"He won't be up for ages," she said, and gestured at a couple of wine bottles by the bin. She poured Andreas's coffee, and sat down at the table, facing him.

"About yesterday," she said. She seemed to wait for him to say something. He didn't.

"I'm sorry about what happened," she finally said, and got up. "I'm not sure I want more than what my imagination can provide."

"Don't apologize," said Andreas. "After all, it's not as though anything happened."

"I have an idea of a marriage," Marthe said. "The way a marriage ought to be. This sort of thing doesn't fit it. It might sound a bit stupid, but there's something unaesthetic about it. I don't want to play the part of the unfaithful wife. I can't."

Marthe stood in the window against the light. Andreas couldn't make out her face very well. She said she had often deceived Jean-Marc in her imagination, and once, it had almost happened. It was when her younger son had started school.

"That's years ago."

She raised her hands and let them sink again. She had suddenly found herself with a lot of time, and not known what to do with it. She had gone into Paris and bought clothes and shoes and kitchenware that she didn't need. She had seen all those young people, and she had suddenly had the feeling that life had passed her by.

"You know, the old story. Married young, and had children right away. Jean-Marc was my first proper relationship."

A couple of times, Marthe had gone to Enghien, one or two Metro stops from Deuil. She wandered around the little lake, had a drink in the casino restaurant, watched the people, and was happy when men turned around to look at her. There she had run into Philippe, the French teacher who had later died of a brain tumor. He told her he went to Enghien every week to play blackjack in the casino.

"I was fascinated. Everyone thought he was going to the library in Paris, to research some book or something, and all the time he was going to the casino. He didn't look anything like a gambler."

Philippe had taken Marthe along to the casino, and explained everything to her. The gambling didn't interest her, but she was fascinated by the atmosphere.

Marthe sat down again, and took a sip from Andreas's coffee.

"Have you ever been to a casino?" she asked. He shook his head.

"The people are completely single-minded. You get the feeling they don't even see each other. If they walk into you, they don't say excuse me. Once, there was an argument about some winnings. Two people both claimed the money as theirs. It wasn't a big sum, but it was as though it was life and death."

Philippe played for small sums. He said he gambled for fun, never winning much, never losing much either. When he was with Marthe, he bet more than he usually did, maybe to impress her. Once, he got lucky, in half an hour he won two thousand francs. They went to the bar and drank champagne.

"Then he suggested we go to a hotel room. I was shocked and ran away."

Philippe started to write her letters. At first, she never answered. Eventually, she got so mad that she wrote to him to stop it. After that they wrote each other regularly. The letters became more and more intimate, they told each other everything about their relationships and their fantasies.

"I wrote him things I've never talked about. Not with anyone. That I had never even given a thought to. It happened while I was writing. We got each other going, stimulated each other."

They met in Enghien a couple of times, but Philippe didn't try to seduce Marthe again. They walked around the lake, not speaking, not touching. They looked at each other, one walked behind the other, or they moved apart and observed each other from a distance. Sometimes they went to the casino and played at the same table, pretending they didn't know each other. Or they went into a bookshop, and followed each other among the shelves, or squeezed past each other, so that their bodies touched fleetingly. When Marthe went to catch her train, Philippe stood on the other platform. She waited for a signal from him, but he just stood there, looking at her. A few days later, he sent her a letter describing how he slept with her, long, obscene descriptions that were completely unerotic, and therefore excited her.

"It was weird. I didn't know I could do that," said Marthe, laughing. "It was like a game."

Then Philippe's wife stumbled upon Marthe's letters. She sent copies to Jean-Marc, and there was a huge fuss, even though Marthe and Philippe had never slept together. Perhaps it would have been easier for Philippe's wife to deal with if we had, said Marthe.

"If we had slept together. She could have laid into me, and the whole thing would have been dealt with. But she must have noticed that we shared something that she would never have."

"Passion?"

Marthe shrugged her shoulders.

"A secret. What do I know."

They had talked once more on the phone. Philippe had been in tears. He was suffering like a dog. Sometimes, later, she thought that was why he had gotten sick. Of course that was nonsense.

"Did you love him?" asked Andreas.

"I don't know," said Marthe, "all I know is that I was ready to leave all of this behind, Jean-Marc, the children, all of it. I don't know if that's love."

"Why didn't you?"

"He didn't want to. He said he would never forgive himself for destroying my family. He never had any children himself. Do you know his wife?"

Andreas nodded. "Did you ever see him again?"

"From a distance. I didn't go to the funeral."

Andreas suddenly felt jealous of Philippe. He couldn't explain it. He liked Marthe all right, but he wasn't in love with her. Perhaps he didn't envy Philippe because of Marthe exactly, so much as because of her love for him. He had always been careful not to be loved too much himself, with every step that a woman had taken toward him, he would take a step away. He hadn't been able to take the turbulence, the dependency.

"I was never for marriage," he said. "You can't own another person."

"This wasn't about possession," said Marthe. "It was more like an addiction, having to be near him."

She said she never wanted to go through something like that again.

"Do you think that was Jean-Marc's revenge? Sleeping with Delphine?"

Marthe shook her head. Those kind of things had happened before. She had noticed it, each time. Anyway, he wasn't like that. He wasn't that subtle. He had probably really fallen in love. Now he was going to have to go through what she had been through. She felt sorry for him, really.

"Are you not afraid he might leave you?"

Marthe didn't reply. She stood up and said she was going to the beach to check up on the kids. Did Andreas fancy coming with her?

The sun was shining, but there was a cool wind off the sea. The children ran squealing into the water, and were thrown back by the waves. Andreas and Marthe sat down on a big rock to watch them. Andreas felt like going for a swim, even though he was shivering in his clothes. He got up and went down to the water. Marthe followed him. They took their shoes off, and let the water wash over their toes.

"You're very quiet," said Marthe.

"I don't know how the children can stand it," said Andreas. "The water's ice cold."

He thought about telling Marthe about his illness, but then he didn't. He mustn't talk about it. Not to anyone. That was his only chance.

Marthe started talking about Philippe again. She said she thought about him every day. It might sound strange, but she felt closer to him now than when they had to break up.

"Now he doesn't belong to anyone anymore. He's free."

"Who was it who said he always wished his lovers were dead?"

"What a terrible sentence," said Marthe. "Great beach conversation."

She called the children. They came out of the water, and ran over to pick up their things. They dried off, and put their clothes on.

When they were smaller, Andreas had sometimes looked after them. He had taken them to the cinema, and watched kids' films with them and enjoyed himself almost as much as they had. He had bought them ice cream and gone to the park with them, where they had run around and played. They had laughed and screamed they were having so much fun. Then, from one moment to the next, they had clammed up and said they wanted to go home. It was as though they were suddenly afraid of him. On the way home, they almost hadn't let him take them by the hand, and when they got home, they had flung themselves at Marthe and buried their heads in her skirts, and Marthe had apologized and said she didn't know what had got into them. What's the matter with you, she had asked, but the children had stood there sullenly and not said anything. Andreas hadn't minded. Perhaps he understood them better than Marthe, or Jean-Marc, who told them to snap out of it.

The older the children got, the more they learned to mask their feelings, to conceal their love, and their dislike and their fear. Now they greeted Andreas amiably when they saw him. They weren't afraid of him anymore, but they had lost their trustingness. They told him about school and tried out their little bit of German on him. How do you do? And Andreas corrected them: How are you? I'm fine. Yes, I'm fine.

Michel, the younger, asked Andreas if he had seen the ships in Brest. Marthe said the big harbor festival was happening again.

"Weren't you here four years ago?"

Andreas nodded, and Michel talked enthusiastically about the *Sedov*, a Russian training ship that they had visited a few days ago.

"It's the biggest sailing ship in the world, a hundred and twenty meters long."

"Michel wants to be a sailor now," Marthe laughed.

"Yes, but only on a sailing ship," said the boy.

"The ship comes from Murmansk. Do you know where that is? It's way up in the north. And then it's always at sea. There's no mama there to look after you."

When they returned to the house, they found Jean-Marc sitting at the kitchen table, reading the sports section of the paper. He had a headache, he said. Marthe said he had only himself to blame for that. The children disappeared upstairs. They must have felt the atmosphere was wrong. Marthe stood behind Jean-Marc, and laid her hands on his shoulders. He turned his head around and looked up at her with a doggish expression. The scene was pathetic and moving at the same time, a couple of drowning people clutching onto one another. Andreas said he would take the train at quarter to four. Marthe said why didn't he stay a couple of days. He shook his head, and she said she would give him a ride to the station.

"I'll do it," said Jean-Marc.

The way back seemed to Andreas to take longer than the way there, even though Jean-Marc drove fast. The winding road followed the bay inland, and then crossed the river and doubled back along the coast. Jean-Marc didn't speak for the entire drive, and Andreas closed his eyes, and dozed off. They got to Brest fully an hour before the train was due to leave.

"Do you want to stop for a drink?" Andreas asked, out of politeness.

They went to a café next to the station. Some of the tables were occupied by sailors in dark blue uniforms.

"They must be from the *Sedov*," said Jean-Marc. "That's a Russian training ship. They're here for the big harbor celebrations."

"Michel was talking about it," said Andreas.

They stood at the bar, drinking coffee. Jean-Marc appeared to want to say something. It took him a couple of run-ups before he could ask his question.

"Are you really together with her?"

"It's nothing serious," said Andreas.

He looked at Jean-Marc, but he had lowered his eyes, and seemed to be looking for words again. Finally he said he didn't hold it against Andreas. He wasn't to know . . .

"Know what?" asked Andreas.

"I don't know what to do," said Jean-Marc. "I can't get over her. And I don't even know what she thinks about me. Did you talk about me?"

"No," lied Andreas.

"What was she like?"

Andreas said he didn't know what Jean-Marc meant.

"What she was like in bed."

Andreas said Delphine had moved in with him for a couple of days. He felt sorry for Jean-Marc. The way he was suffering, and didn't even try to conceal it. There was something humiliating about a man of his age not having more self-control.

"I'm crazy about her," said Jean-Marc. "Do you really think she'll sleep with anyone?"

"That's rubbish," said Andreas. "She said you showed her pictures of your kids."

"Oh, so you did talk about me. What did she say?"

"She said you were a moron."

Jean-Marc's head jerked up. He looked questioningly at Andreas, then he lowered his head, and said he'd better go. His voice sounded washed out, almost inaudible. See you soon, said Andreas. Jean-Marc raised his hand in greeting, and walked out. Andreas watched him cross the road, get in his car, and sit there for a moment, quite still, before driving off. Andreas asked himself how he had struck up this friendship with Jean-Marc, why he had spent so much time with him, when he was someone to whom he felt totally indifferent.

He was back in Paris by eight o'clock. He didn't feel well, and he took a taxi from the station. There were a couple of messages on the answering machine. The first was from Nadia. She said she forgave him, and then she went straight into a new round of reproaches. He wiped the message before he'd got to the end. The second was from the doctor's office. A woman's voice asked him to call back. It was a completely unemotional voice. Andreas deleted the second message as well.

He started tidying up his things. First, he stashed everything in cardboard boxes that he brought up from the basement. Then he started throwing away more and more. He had taken the books off the shelves and sorted them into two piles. He looked through them a second time, and pulled out a Jack London book and the book about the au pair girl. All the others went in the junk. He carried the full trash bags out into the corridor. It was eleven o'clock. He felt exhausted. He lay down on the bed without undressing or turning off the light.

In the middle of the night he was awakened by a fit of coughing. He got up to go to the bathroom. He felt cold. He turned on the central heating, slid under the blankets with his clothes on, and turned off the light. The stand-by lights glowed in the dark. One day, when there are no more people left in the world, he thought, there will still be stand-by lights glowing, and the clocks on electronic devices will continue to tell the time that no longer exists, until the last power plants have switched off and the last batteries are dry.

In the morning, he woke up late. It was hot in the bedroom, and the air felt dry. He had another fit of coughing that seemed to go on for ever. After he'd drunk his coffee, he felt a little better. He went back to tidying. The things he'd stowed in cardboard boxes the night before he now threw away.

At noon, he carted all the garbage bags down to the yard. He went to McDonald's and bought something to eat. When he came back, there was a message on the answering machine. It was the realtor, to say he had found some potential buyers for the apartment, and that he would be there in fifteen minutes to show them around. No sooner had Andreas heard the end of the message than the bell rang, and the key turned in the lock.

He had thought Andreas was on vacation, the realtor said. Andreas said he had come home earlier than he'd expected. He was just clearing up in the apartment. They should have a look around, by all means. The realtor introduced him to the potential buyers, who were a couple from Perpignan by the name of Cordelier.

The woman was pregnant, and looked rather teary. The man had black hair, a tanned face, and a brutal expression. He said he worked for a wholesale florist, and had been moved to Paris to give things there a bit of a shaking-up.

"He's been promoted to assistant director," said the woman, visibly proud of her husband.

Andreas stayed in the kitchen while the realtor showed the couple around the apartment. He heard little exclamations of delight. Finally the three of them arrived in the kitchen.

"It's such a bijou apartment," said the woman.

"A bit on the small side," said the man.

The realtor said they wouldn't find anything bigger for that money, not in that neighborhood.

"Prices have risen steeply these past years," he said, "and they're continuing to climb. The apartment is a great investment."

Andreas was surprised that they didn't ask him why he was moving. The woman asked about playgrounds, kindergartens, and schools in the vicinity. Andreas said he didn't have kids. There were a couple of little parks nearby, said the realtor, and the cemetery of Montmartre was just around the corner. Of course, it was nothing like Perpignan.

"Your first?" he asked.

The woman nodded eagerly, and said they'd been married just a year. She leaned against her husband, and he wrapped his arms around her neck and kissed her on the cheek. It looked as though he was strangling her.

"I love the furniture," said the woman, "it's very stylish. Don't you think, Hervé?"

"We've been staying with my wife's parents up until now," the man said.

"They have an enormous house," she said, "and a big garden with old trees."

Andreas said he didn't need the furniture anymore. If they wanted any of it, that was something they could talk about. Suddenly, the woman's expression turned sad. The man put his hand on her belly, and said everything would be fine.

"It's all so new to me," she said, "the baby and the city, and all the things we need to get."

"Just take a look around," said the realtor. "I'll leave you alone, so you can discuss it together in peace."

The couple took another turn around the apartment. The realtor nodded at Andreas and made the thumbs-up sign. Then he rubbed the fingers of his right hand together.

"The fellow's a bit dim," he said quietly. "The company he works for belongs to her parents. That's where the money's coming from."

Andreas offered him coffee, but the realtor declined. He put his hand on his stomach, and asked if he could have a glass of water. They waited in silence. After a while, Andreas stepped out into the corridor and looked in at the living room. The couple were standing by the window, kissing. The man had dropped to his knees, he had pushed up the woman's skirts, and was stroking the inside of her thigh. Andreas crept back to the kitchen. The realtor looked at him questioningly, and Andreas made a face.

"It really is a lovely apartment," said the woman, coming back into the kitchen. The man was still in the corridor, and seemed to be studying the fuse box.

"Well then, shall we?" said the realtor. He said they had another apartment to see. He shook Andreas's hand. "You'll hear from me."

The hamburger was stone cold and tasted disgusting, but Andreas ate it anyway. Then he went and lay down. He lay on the sofa, and imagined the Cordeliers moving into his apartment. He stood in the yard, looking up at the lit windows behind which the family was living. The kid went up to the window, and pulled the curtain aside, and looked out. He was a little boy of about five. While Andreas watched him, he seemed to grow and get older. His mother came up behind him, pushed him away from the window, and drew the curtain shut. Her face looked worn and tired. Then Monsieur Cordelier—Hervé—came down into the yard. He was carrying two bags full of empty bottles. He dropped the bottles in one of the green recycling containers. He said something to himself, and laughed out loud. His laugh sounded rather unpleasant. Then the boy was playing ball in the yard. Someone opened a window and told him to clear out. The boy walked through the yard. He tried not to step on the cracks between the paving slabs. He skipped from stone to stone. His mother called down to him to run and play with the others. The yard opened out, and a wide landscape appeared. Andreas was on his bicycle. The road was as straight as a die. He was heading into the wind, and seemed not to be moving at all, but when he turned around, the wind was still in his face. He got off, and pushed the bicycle across the flat plain. He felt he wasn't moving. In the sky, dark clouds slid by, but he knew it wouldn't rain, not yet. Then it did rain. Andreas was in his room in the attic.

The rain was pelting on the skylight. It was cool in the room. Andreas lay down on the bed. He was reading a book, but the words blurred before his eyes. He was on a desert island with a couple of other children. He didn't know how they had gotten there. They were on the beach. When it got dark, they went into the forest, which was a tropical forest. They came to a crumbling tenement house, a bombed-out ruin. The children stood in front of the house and debated what to do. Andreas seemed to know the other children. They were older than him.

The telephone woke him. He looked at his watch, it was five. He hesitated for a moment, and then picked up. It was the realtor. He said things were looking good. The Cordeliers were very interested. The woman had tried to get him to lower the price, but he hadn't budged. Her parents were coming up from Perpignan at the weekend, to look at the apartment. Would he be there? Andreas said he didn't know.

"I know these kind of people," said the realtor. "If they like the place, they'll move fast."

Andreas emptied out the cupboard in the landing. He was surprised he had so many things he had completely forgotten about. Whole boxes full of notes, letters, records. He leafed through them, stopped to read the occasional page, and then threw everything away without hesitating. A couple of cassettes he had recorded years ago, carefully writing down the tracks, he kept for a long drive sometime.

He found a box full of letters and postcards from friends, and from his mother. Letters she had written to him during his time doing national service, in which she talked about ordinary day-to-day things, illnesses, excursions, visits. The last traces of a life that was snuffed out. Traces that weren't traces, just words without any weight. At the bottom of the box were some letters from Fabienne. He must have collected them together some time, wrapped them in packing paper, and sealed the parcel. He broke the seal and read a couple of the letters. Their banality astonished him.

Fabienne wrote to say she had a paper to write about *The Magic Mountain* by Thomas Mann, and had he ever read it? She had been out to a restaurant with some friends where people ate with their bare hands, like the ancient Gauls. She had met three Americans who had wanted to take her picture. Why had she written him that? One October, she had gone to Normandy with friends and gone swimming, even though the water was cold. Another time, she had eaten oysters and gotten sick. Andreas was surprised at the many friends and girlfriends she mentioned. With one letter was a photograph showing Fabienne in the middle of a group of young people. They were wearing colored paper hats and laughing drunkenly at the camera. On the back of the photograph she had written: "Best wishes for the New Year." Best wishes for a new year that was long gone, and that Andreas couldn't even recall. He wrapped up Fabienne's letters in the packing paper, and put the parcel on the table. He threw away the other letters.

In another carton he found a pile of his old appointment diaries, little books that left about a line of space for each day. He had never kept a diary as such, the thought of keeping a record of his life always seemed to him absurd. It was only these calendars he had kept, where the years were summed up in very few words, the names of people he had met, vacation places, dates of exams and doctors' appointments. In his first years in the city he had written down the titles of all the films he had seen, the restaurants he had eaten in. With time, he had gotten more and more casual and remiss. He always went to the same restaurants anyway, and the films he went to see weren't important. His meetings with Nadia and Sylvie were so regular that he didn't need to write down dates and times. Over the last few years, there were more and more months where the calendar had remained blank, where it contained no traces.

Slipped into one of them was a list of all the women he had slept with. He read the names. In some cases he couldn't even put a face to the name, or only after long thought. The list was a couple of years old. He added a few more names, then crumpled up the sheet and threw it away.

One list among many, he thought. His life was an endless sequence of lessons, of cigarettes, meals, cinema visits, meetings with women or friends who basically didn't mean anything to him, incoherent lists of little events. Sometimes he had given up trying to get the whole thing to make sense, trying to look for sense on it. The less the events in his life had to do with one another, the more interchangeable they had become. Sometimes he appeared to himself like a tourist, racing from one sight to the next in a city he doesn't even know the name of. Loads of beginnings that had nothing to do with the end, with his death, which in turn would mean nothing beyond the fact that he had run out of time.

At the weekend, Mme Cordelier's parents came and looked at the apartment. They liked it, and that same day drew up a purchase agreement. The Cordeliers wanted to have the walls painted, and the floors sanded. They didn't want to keep any of the furniture.

The realtor said they wouldn't sign the final contract for another six weeks at the earliest. Andreas said he would be moving out in a couple of days, and going abroad. The realtor said he could give someone power of attorney to represent him in front of the notary. The money would be transferred to his account after the sale.

On Monday, the furniture dealer came and picked up the furniture. He was about to pick up the statue of the Huntress when Andreas said he'd prefer to keep it. The junk dealer said it was valueless. He offered Andreas a sum for the furniture that was far too low. Andreas argued with him for the sake of it, and managed to get a little more money out of him.

Everything he owned now fitted into a suitcase, the same red artificial leather suitcase he had arrived with in the city eighteen years ago: a few clothes, toiletries, a sleeping bag, Fabienne's letters, the cassettes, and the two books he had decided to hold on to. He wasn't even taking his address book. He felt light, free of all his ballast. It was as though he had been asleep all those years, grown numb like a limb that hadn't moved for ages. Now he felt that same pleasant pain that you feel when the blood shoots back into an arm or a leg. He was still alive, he could move.

That night was Andreas's last in the apartment. He spread the sleeping bag out on the floor as on the first nights he had spent there, and, just as then, the apartment felt strange to him and a little frightening. He slept badly. When he woke up, it was just getting light. His footfall echoed in the empty rooms, and his cough sounded quite threatening. Andreas went up to the window and threw it open. It had rained a little overnight, and the cement slabs in the yard all glistened darkly. He lit a cigarette and smoked it without enjoyment. He watched a blackbird whistling and skipping from branch to branch. When he shut the window, he frightened it and it flew off. He had meant to stay a little longer to take his leave of the place that he would never see again, but suddenly it no longer interested him. It wasn't possible to say good-bye to anything or anyone, he thought. The last look was just like the first, and memory was no more than one of many possibilities.

He wrapped the statuette in one of the curtains he had taken down from the windows. Then, without a last look back, he left the apartment. In the mailbox he found a couple of flyers and a letter, which he pocketed without looking for the sender's name. He thought he should have gotten in touch with the post office before leaving, but then he had no forwarding address, and didn't know where he was going. Presumably his mail would be returned to sender, with a little stamp, *Addressee Unknown*.

He dropped the key in the mailbox, as he'd agreed with the realtor. When the front door shut behind him, he stopped for a moment, uncertain which way to go. In the end he went the way he had gone almost every day for the last few years. He walked down the street to the Boulevard de Clichy. At the bank, he withdrew all the money he had in his account. Then he walked on, straight on, to the Boulevard de Magenta, and from there to the Gare du Nord. When he reached the hospital, he walked a little faster, as though afraid someone might recognize him and stop him. Behind the station, he was approached by a woman of about his own age.

"Excuse me," she said, as their eyes met.

Andreas raised his hand to ward her off. Though the woman didn't look poor, he was certain she would ask him for money. He wanted to say something, but his voice failed him. Only his mouth moved. The woman mouthed something back to him, and they each went on their own way. Maybe she just wanted to ask me the time, he thought, or directions to somewhere. He turned around. The woman was nowhere in sight.

He took the train to Deuil. He was later than usual, the rush hour was over, but the train was full just the same, and he had to stand in the corridor with his suitcase and his wrapped statue. In Deuil, he didn't walk to school, but took the other direction.

The used car dealer would have preferred to sell Andreas a different car than the old 2CV. He said he had higher performance models on offer, for only a slightly higher price.

"It's a collector's item," he said, "what you're paying for is the name. Let me show you something a bit sportier."

"I am a collector," said Andreas. He said he would pay cash. He took a wad of banknotes from his pocket, and counted out the money in front of the astonished seller.

"Can I take it right away?"

The salesman said he had to get registration papers issued for it first. That would take at least five days. Andreas asked if there was a hotel anywhere nearby. The salesman didn't know of any hotels here. There were the spa hotels in Enghien, but they were expensive. If he didn't want to go back into the city, there were plenty of cheap places to stay on the *Périphérique*.

Andreas took a taxi to the Porte de la Chapelle. Right on the motorway, he found a cheap Etap hotel, and took a room. He said he wasn't sure how long he'd be staying, and paid for one night.

It wasn't midday yet, and he had to wait until his room was ready. He sat in the lobby. Along a wall were machines for drinks and candy, and one that sold maps, dictionaries, toothbrushes, and condoms. Everything a man could wish for, thought Andreas. A couple of young blacks stood around in front of the machines, talking loudly. Not hotel guests, he thought.

Andreas watched a couple with their son, standing at the reception desk, talking to the clerk. The father was not much older than he was, but he looked tired and unhealthy. He was wearing jeans and an old-fashioned knitted sweater, over a little beer belly. The son, who was as old as Andreas's pupils, was almost as tall as his father. He was thin and pale and had a spotty face. The mother had short, bleached hair. Andreas was sure they were German. The man looked lost and uncertain, and the woman ill-tempered. The porter was talking to them a little exasperatedly.

Andreas went up to the reception desk, and asked, in German, if he could help. The man looked at him in surprise, and then explained that he had thought the car park was included in the price for the room. Andreas translated. The porter said the price for the underground garage was separate. It wasn't a very great amount, but the father seemed not to have been expecting the extra expense. The family didn't look well-off, presumably they were on a budget, and maybe had spent more money than they had.

The woman said once or twice they didn't have to stand for it. She looked disapprovingly at her husband, as though he was to blame for the mix-up. For a brief moment, Andreas thought of paying for it himself, but he knew it wouldn't help in the end.

The room was small, and you could tell that all possible economies had been made on it. There was a toilet, but no bath. The door to the shower was glass, and opened directly into the room, the washbasin was mounted on the wall just next to it. Tucked behind the head of the double bed was a narrow foldaway cot for a third person.

Andreas imagined the German family spending the night in a room like this, the parents in the bed, the boy above them in the cot. He imagined them showering in the morning, the nakedness and the lack of space, the boy's embarrassment as he treated his face with an acne preparation without being able to lock the bathroom door, the way he did at home. He imagined them traipsing through Paris, looking for the beauty of the city, and he asked himself whether they had found it. Their feet were hurting, they stopped for lunch in a restaurant with a German menu, where the waiter cheated them. Then there was an argument, because the parents wanted to go to a museum, and the boy didn't. And then, when they asked him what he wanted to do, he couldn't say anything.

Andreas was glad he had missed all that. He was glad he had never had a family. It was as near as he wanted to get, the times when his pupils went up to him at the end of class, and told him of their problems, and when he called the parents, and tried to mediate. Once or twice a pupil had even slept on his sofa, when home had become completely impossible.

He stood by the window and looked out at the many lanes of the highway. You couldn't open the windows. They were soundproofed; only rarely you could hear the stifled sound of a car horn or an especially loud gear-change.

Andreas had been in his room since midday. He spent hours watching the traffic, sometimes the cars drove very close together, sometimes a little less, and then toward evening they solidified in columns, and now they were just starting to crawl forward again. The drivers had switched on their headlights. Night fell. They will drive like this forever, he thought, the traffic will never get any less. He thought about his death, or tried to think about it. But his life had been so uneventful that he couldn't imagine his death. He could only see himself lying in some hospital somewhere. And then the road again, the numberless cars. *God Almighty has counted them up, to be sure that none is missing.* The stars, the grains of sand, the sheep in His herd. Even when he was a child, Andreas hadn't believed in that.

Fear, fear wasn't a thought. Fear seemed to come from outside. When Andreas thought of being sick he didn't feel fear. He was desperate, confused, he struggled with himself, he reproached himself. Whereas fear came suddenly, without warning. It was like a darkening of his thoughts. Fear made it impossible to breathe, crushed his body until he felt ready to explode and break apart into a fine spray consisting of billions and billions of tiny droplets, spinning into the void.

In the morning, the whole hotel stank of disinfectant. For breakfast there was coffee in plastic cups, the bread was soggy, and the orange juice watered.

Andreas left the hotel. The sky was gray, but it wasn't cold. He strolled through the neighborhood. Not since he had first come to Paris, had he ever been out here. He had driven through St. Denis every day, but only ever seen the huge residential blocks from the train window, and in between them streets with dinky single-family homes in postage-stamp gardens, and further out, near the Stade de France, the new commercial district that had sprung up over the last few years.

Not far from the hotel was a cemetery, behind a high wall. Next to it was a funeral parlor, with a display of various sample gravestones in different shades of marble. In the window was a poster for their summer sale item, which was a stone in pale granite, and a stele with your own choice of top, all at a very low price. Andreas entered the cemetery. A man in a tracksuit came out of the toilet right beside the entrance, and walked past him. Andreas felt reminded of a joke he had once heard. It was something to do with death and tracksuits. He couldn't remember how it went. A plane crash, maybe? He walked slowly between the rows of graves. There were some in which whole families were buried together. The lists of names were like family sagas, the names of the oldest were barely decipherable, and the newest had a brassy gleam. He stopped in front of one particularly ugly grave with heavy iron chains and a roof copied from some Greek temple. He read the names and dates. Between the Fifties and the Eighties no one in the family seemed to have died, but then in the space of a few years, there had been five deaths. There was a withered bunch of flowers on the grave, so there had to be descendants, people who remembered the dead. There was room on the slab for another one or two names anyway.

Andreas left the cemetery, and walked on through the *quartier*. He was astonished how clean and tidy everything looked. He read the names by the doorbells, foreign-sounding names, he couldn't tell where they came from. Some sounded Arabic, others Eastern European or Asian. There was almost no one on the streets. There were no shops, only a community center with public baths and showers. In the windows of a kindergarten hung some colored drawings, a dozen terrifying android beings all with extra-large heads, that looked exactly the same.

At noon Andreas was back in the hotel. He paid the room for another night. He had bought a few magazines, and spent the afternoon lying on his bed, reading articles about the most scenic golf courses in the world, and about plastic surgery, and about film festivals. In a women's magazine he found a list of a hundred tips for good sex. Try to look attractive at all times, comb your hair and freshen your lipstick. Small gifts spread happiness. Complimenting your partner's physique will intensify your pleasure and his.

He fell asleep. When he awoke, it was nighttime. He felt restless, he knew he wouldn't be able to sleep anymore. He left the hotel, and prowled through the neighborhood. After a while, he got to the new business centers that he had been able to see every day from the train. A few of them were only just completed, and not yet occupied. The glass facades had a blackish sheen in the light of the streetlamps. There were security cameras everywhere, but not a soul around.

On the way back, he passed the cemetery again, which was closed now. He wondered who would visit his grave, who would think of him when he was dead. Walter and Bettina, maybe. And apart from them? From time to time someone would read the inscription on his stone, and calculate the age at which he had died, and think he didn't get to grow very old. And in twenty years' time, Walter or one of his children would sign a form, and Andreas's grave would be cleared, and there would be no more trace of him.

Andreas stayed at the hotel for a week. Every morning after breakfast, he paid for another night, and then he headed straight back upstairs. When the chambermaid came to do his room, he would wait out in the hall until she was finished. He slept a lot, and tried to read, and spent whole afternoons motionless on his bed, lost in vague drifts of thought. Sometimes he felt so weak, he was barely able to get up and put his clothes on, and at others he paced through the neighborhood, as though he might be able to escape his illness that way. Once or twice he thought of calling the doctor's office because he could no longer stand the uncertainty, but then he put off the call until office hours were safely over.

On the day he was able to collect his car, he felt better. He got up early, showered, and packed his things. Then he called Delphine and asked if he could see her. She asked him where he was. She sounded sleepy. He said he could be with her in an hour. On the bus to Deuil he wrote a text message to Sylvie. She had sent him a message the day before, and asked him in her telegraphic style how he was feeling and what he was up to. He hadn't replied. Now he wrote to say he was doing fine, and he wished her a nice summer. No sooner had he sent it off, than he got her reply. Sylvie wished him happy holidays and sent him a hug.

At half past nine, Andreas was standing outside Delphine's house. It took a while from when he'd rung the bell to the buzz of the door opener. In the courtyard, Andreas looked up, but he couldn't remember which window was Delphine's. Slowly he climbed the stairs. When he was on the third floor, he could hear a door opening above him. Delphine stood there on the landing. She was in her nightie, but that didn't seem to bother her.

"What do you want?" she asked. She looked serious, but not hostile.

"You left your toothbrush behind."

"Don't play games with me."

"I'm sorry," said Andreas, "about what I said."

"And that means everything's all right?"

Delphine looked at his suitcase. She smiled, and asked him if he was intending to move in with her. Andreas said he had to talk to her. Delphine let him in, and led the way into the kitchen. He sat down, she remained standing. She stood very close to him. He put out his hands and grabbed her around the waist. Through the thin material he could feel the warmth of her body. She took a step away from him, and said she was going to have a quick shower and get dressed. While she was gone, Andreas poured himself a glass of water, and drank it in quick gulps.

"To see you sitting there like a poor sinner," said Delphine, returning. She was wearing the same dress she had worn at their last meeting.

"Weren't you going to go to the seaside?" asked Andreas.

"Not till the end of the week," replied Delphine. "But I'm not quite sure whether I'm going yet. My parents are being annoying."

She hadn't found an apartment, she said. She no longer even felt sure she wanted to go to Versailles.

"I got my exam results last week. I passed. Now I've got a guaranteed job for life. I'm not sure how I feel about that."

Andreas asked her what else she could do. Delphine looked at him in a bored way, and said that was exactly what her parents were saying. She didn't know. She felt too young to be tied down like that. She wanted to live.

"I'm going to Switzerland," said Andreas. "Do you fancy coming with me?"

Delphine seemed less surprised by the question than he was. She asked why didn't he go to the sea with her. He didn't say anything. She thought about it for a moment, and then she said OK, she would come. She had never been to Switzerland. When were they leaving?

"I bought a car," said Andreas. "I can go and collect it today."

Delphine said she had to take care of a few things, and make some necessary purchases. They arranged to meet at four o'clock. Andreas said he would pick her up.

When Delphine saw the 2CV, she suggested they take her car instead. Andreas shook his head.

"My best friend had a 2CV," he said. "When I was young, we used to drive to the lake in it."

They rounded Paris on the *Périphérique*. The sun was high in the sky, the city swam in a milky haze. The sky and the buildings were one and the same color, only different in shadings. The roads were choked with holiday traffic. Delphine had opened the roof, and turned on the radio. They were listening to a jazz station, and Andreas tried to guess the titles of the standards they played.

"When I was pretty new in Paris, I saw Chet Baker in the *New Morning*," he said. "He was incredibly thin and hollow-cheeked. He sat slumped on a barstool, with his trumpet jammed between his legs. Then he started singing, very quietly, and with a cracked voice. I can't remember the name of the piece, 'The Touch of Your Lips' or 'She Was Too Good to Me,' but I can still hear his voice today. After a few bars he breaks off, and makes an angry gesture, and the band starts over. His performance was like the echo of an echo. Shortly after, he died."

He said he preferred Chet Baker's late recordings to his early ones. It was no longer a matter of getting the perfect sound. There were cracks, little mistakes and imprecisions. The music was more alive, failure was a possibility, even a certainty. Delphine asked him who this Chet Baker was. She said she didn't listen to jazz much.

When they came off the *Périphérique* at the Porte d'Italie, Delphine asked whether they shouldn't rather drive to Italy or the south of France.

"We can do whatever we want," she said. "We're completely free."

Andreas didn't say anything. It was a long time since he had last driven, and he had to concentrate on the traffic. Delphine leaned back and looked out the window. Later, they listened to the cassettes Andreas had packed, rock music he had liked once, and chansons that Delphine thought were horrible. Andreas sang along to Francis Cabrel:

> *J'aimerais quand même te dire*
> *tout ce que j'ai pu écrire*
> *je l'ai puisé à l'encre de tes yeux*

Delphine laughed and said her eyes were brown, not blue. Andreas said the music took him back to his youth. At the time he had written poetry when he was in love.

"Erotic poetry?"

"Sentimental would be more like it."

"I wouldn't have thought you capable of that," said Delphine. "A spark of love within a frozen heart."

She said it in jest, but Andreas was a little surprised, just the same. He had never thought of himself as a cold person, but it wasn't the first time he had heard such an accusation. *C'était l'hiver dans le fond de son coeur*, sang Francis Cabrel. Andreas remembered how the song had moved him once, and how he had joined the singer in grieving for the death of the girl who kills herself on the eve of her twentieth birthday. Delphine said she couldn't bear it, it was too mawkish. She pushed the eject button, and pulled another cassette from the plastic bag at her feet. She put it in, there was a moment's silence, and then a woman's warm voice. *Part seven: Reflexive pronouns.*

Andreas wanted to take the cassette out, but Delphine put her hand over his, and they listened to the woman slowly and clearly speak the examples.

Tomorrow I shall see you again. Tomorrow you will see me again. Tomorrow we will see you again. Tomorrow you will see us again. The parents see their children again. The children see their parents again.

Then a man's voice, equally warm, intoned:

My day. I get up at half past five in the morning. I always get up at that time, because I have to be in the office by eight. It is only on weekends that I can sleep in. After getting up, I go to the bathroom, clean my teeth and shower, first warm, and then cold at the finish. After that, I feel thoroughly awake, and well. Then I get dressed and comb my hair. I go to the kitchen to have breakfast. I make myself some coffee, eat bread with jam, or cheese or sausage . . .

The man's voice had something strangely cheerful about it. It sounded as though he had yielded completely to the course of such days and years, a destiny without subordinate clauses.

"I me, you you," said Delphine, and then she repeated it, running it together like one word.

"You are the I-me," she said.

"I-you," said Andreas. He took the cassette out of the player, and the radio came back on. He asked her if she had understood the text. Most of it, she said, she wasn't surprised no one wanted to learn German if that was how they taught it. Sausage for breakfast.

At Beaune, they left the Autoroute. A little outside the center, Andreas found an Ibis hotel, and parked.

"I imagined my holiday a bit more romantic than this," said Delphine.

Andreas said he didn't feel like driving into the town. Anyway, they had an early start tomorrow.

They took a room, and went back out to pick up their suitcases.

"They've even got a pool," said Delphine. "What have you got in that bundle?"

She tugged at the curtain, in which Andreas had wrapped the little statue.

"Don't," he said, and shut the trunk.

Delphine thought she would swim before supper, to cool off. Andreas said he would have a drink meanwhile. It was not a large swimming pool, surrounded by a fence, and just a few steps from the terrace of the hotel restaurant. Andreas sat at a table at the edge of the terrace, and ordered a Ricard. It didn't seem to bother Delphine that the diners could watch her as she climbed into the water and swam a few lengths. She came out, squeezed the water from her short hair with one hand, and dried herself. Then she wrapped herself in the towel, and came up to Andreas's table. She sat down, and looked at the menu.

"Do you want to eat here?"

"Don't mind."

"Well, then, let's go somewhere else."

Andreas went up to the room with Delphine, and watched her as she got changed. She put on a little green skirt of rough cotton and a thin black cardigan. She went into the bathroom, and came back with pink lipstick on. Andreas had never seen her with lipstick on. He said she looked nice. He wondered what she liked about him, or what she had liked about Jean-Marc.

They walked along the main road, heading for the town center. They passed a lot of hotels, a shopping center, and roundabouts decorated with wine barrels and vines.

The old center was all done up. Every other house was a restaurant or a wine cellar. Delphine wanted to look at the cathedral. The nave was dark. If you pushed a button, some lights came on that lit up the altar and one especially noteworthy chapel. Delphine lit a candle. Andreas asked who that was for. No one in particular she said, just on account.

"Now God owes me."

"I wonder what sort of miracle you'll get for one euro," said Andreas.

The town was full of tourists, they choked the streets and occupied the tables of the garden restaurants. It was all too noisy and full for Andreas. Finally he said they had passed a cafeteria near the shopping center. Delphine protested, but in the end she gave in.

When they were back at the shopping center, they saw that the cafeteria was due to close in half an hour. The woman behind the counter told them they would have to hurry. They picked up a first course at the counter, and ordered the dish of the day. Delphine chose a bottle of wine.

Not many of the tables were occupied. There were a few men by themselves, a group of Japanese tourists, and a woman with her three children. She took two of them to the bathroom. The third, a boy of about seven, stayed behind on his own. He sat there very still, lost in thought. Suddenly Andreas felt enormous sympathy for him. He felt like going up to him and speaking to him or buying him an ice cream. Then the mother came back with the other two.

"Don't you like it?" asked Delphine.

Andreas said he had been thinking about how they used to eat in restaurants like this one when he was a child.

"I could never decide what I wanted. My parents pressured me, and in the end I always ordered the wrong thing. I had been looking forward to going so much, and it was always a disappointment in the end."

Delphine said going out to eat had always been a treat for her. It hadn't happened often, and her mother wasn't an especially good cook.

The hotel restaurant was shut. A group of girls were sitting in the lobby, talking in German. Presumably they were here on a school trip. They talked and laughed together loudly.

Andreas recalled the graduation trip for his class in high school. They had gone to Paris, four days of sightseeing, three nights in a cheap tourist hotel. For the first time, he remembered Paris as he found it then—not the city in which he had spent the subsequent eighteen years. It was a big city in autumn. The air was as clear as glass, and yet a strange fog seemed to hang over everything, impeding your vision, and shading the edges of what you saw. People moved a little more slowly here, as though they were in an atmosphere that was heavier than air.

Their hotel was somewhere in the northwest of the city, a part Andreas hadn't been back to since. He remembered the name of the Metro station, La Fourche—a line divided there. Their class teacher had been nervous, and hadn't let the boys and girls out of his sight. Only rarely had they had an hour or two for themselves, after sightseeing trips and museum visits, and before supper. Then Andreas had set out on his own, exploring the quarter in ever-widening circles.

He remembered feeling extraordinarily happy to be standing in a bistro between two men stopping off for a drink on their way home, watching youths playing pinball, and women clicking rapidly past outside the big windows. It was the freest Andreas had ever felt.

He got the map out of the car. In the room he studied the route they would be taking tomorrow. Delphine was in the bathroom. He tried to imagine her as his wife, the two of them newly married, and on their honey-moon. The fantasy both calmed and excited him.

Delphine came out of the bathroom in a short nightie of flowered terrycloth and got into bed. Andreas undressed, turned the light out, and lay down beside her. When he put his hand on her thigh, she said she would get a condom. He held her tight. What if I get pregnant, she asked. He didn't say anything. They made love in the dark, more energetically than usual, and without exchanging a word. Then Delphine switched on the bedside lamp, and went to the bathroom. Andreas heard the faucet running, and then the flush, and then water again. When Delphine came back at last, he said they would have to be careful not to fall in love. Delphine jumped on him, and they wrestled together. She sat on his belly, and grabbed his wrists and pushed them down on the mattress.

"You are such an idiot," she said.

He wanted to say something back, but she kissed him on the mouth, and bit his lip until he freed himself, threw her down on her back, and held her down.

"Stop it," he said. "You'll hurt me."

She tried to free herself, but couldn't. Her breath was coming hard, and she repeated that he was an idiot.

"All right," said Andreas. "That's enough."

Around noon the next day they crossed the border into Switzerland. During the entire drive, Delphine talked about her childhood and teen years, about the police barracks she had grown up in. She had always lived in pretty reduced circumstances, and with lots of other families with children. It had been like a big commune. All the fathers had had the same job, and the mothers were in and out of each other's apartments, drinking coffee and chatting. When Andreas asked her if it had been a happy childhood, she hesitated.

"Sometimes happy, sometimes not. Moving was always tough. Losing my friends. It's only a few that I met up with again, years later, in other barracks."

The best thing had been the summer vacation, three or four weeks on the Atlantic coast.

"That was Paradise. There were always the same people there. All year, we would be out of touch, but when we arrived there, there they all were again. We were like brothers and sisters, swimming in the sea together, and playing on the beach. Those summers were never-ending. In the evenings, there were parties, people eating, drinking, dancing. All of them together. Fireworks sometimes."

Once, there had been a forest fire, that was when she was about ten or so. The fire had approached to within a few miles of the campsite, but she hadn't been scared.

"People assumed it was arson. For days they talked about nothing else. But I still remember thinking nothing can happen to us. No one will find us here."

It was at the campsite that Delphine had learned to swim and surf, and this was where she fell in love for the first time as well. It had been a brief episode, and hadn't lasted beyond the summer.

"We met at night on the dunes. He was clumsy, and I didn't have much of a clue either. Actually, it was pretty horrible, sand everywhere, and afraid of being caught. After that everything changed. Suddenly, everyone had a boyfriend or a girlfriend, and our group fell apart. One year, I didn't go at all. I went hitchhiking around Europe with a girlfriend. But since then I've gone every year. Even if it was just for a few days. My old friends still go. Some have joined the police themselves, married, had babies, and now the kids are playing together. That's the way of it."

She asked Andreas when he had fallen in love for the first time. He said it was so long ago, he could hardly remember.

"Where are we going anyway?" asked Delphine, after they had passed Basel.

"To my village," said Andreas. "We'll be there in a couple of hours."

"And what will we do there? Is there something worth seeing?"

Andreas shrugged his shoulders. The landscape was quite pretty, he said.

The nearer they came to the village, the more unsure he was whether it was a good idea to have taken Delphine with him. He didn't know himself what he had in mind. To see his brother, his parents' grave, maybe Fabienne. And then? He would have enough money from the sale of the apartment to live for a couple of years. But did he really want to go back to his village? He thought of fish that go back to the place they were born, in order to die. Or was it to spawn? Or both together? He couldn't remember.

And what if Delphine really was pregnant? Andreas had never been particularly careful where birth control was concerned. For a long time he had thought he was infertile, then one day Nadia told him she had aborted a baby of his. She said it in her typical, indifferent way, which she only ever set aside when speaking about politics, or her ex. It didn't seem to have occurred to her that Andreas might want the child, though in fact he was relieved she had taken the decision away from him.

She had spoken, if he remembered correctly, not about a baby but about a condition. What had depressed him at the time wasn't that the baby would never be born, it was that he seemed to accept it so easily. He had long since abandoned the idea that there might be some turning point in his life. Some time long ago he had chosen a certain path, a certain direction, and there was no going back on it. Even now, when he had given everything up, it was as though there was only one possible way. He didn't have the feeling of freedom that he had had as a very young man. Everything was already decided. A baby wouldn't change that either. He was reminded of what the doctor had said, that there was no sense in talking about odds. It was either-or. People were born, people died. It happened, or it didn't happen. In the end, it barely mattered.

He looked at Delphine, sitting beside him silent and with eyes closed. He wondered what she was thinking or dreaming of. What had he dreamed of when he was her age? He did the math. It would have been at the end of his first year in Paris.

He came off the Autoroute a little earlier than necessary, and they took country roads through tiny villages, consisting of no more than a couple of farms apiece, a pub, sometimes a church. The road led straight along a wide valley. Only a very few cars met them, and once a boy on a tractor, pulling a mower. Either side of the road were meadows and fields and apple orchards. It was a hot afternoon. Andreas remembered afternoons like it, that felt like holidays, brooding heat on the land and the air every bit as hot and still as the earth. Over everything was a hazy brightness, in which even the shadows looked somehow pale. The forests too were silent, but for an occasional crackle, as if there was a fire burning somewhere.

They crossed the river, which was very low. It had been straightened a long time ago, and flowed in a line across the plain. Andreas stopped next to an old wooden covered bridge.

"What's up?" asked Delphine.

"I just wanted to stretch my legs a bit."

When he was a child, the road had gone over that bridge. Now it was closed to traffic. They crossed it on foot. Delphine took Andreas's hand, but let it go after a few steps.

On the other side was a wooded slope and an abandoned inn, that had once been a customs house. After the bridge was closed to traffic, a small circus had made the place its winter quarters. Barns had been erected, and paddocks for the animals. There was a half-collapsed caravan by the side of the road, and some rusty tubs for a number involving lions. The terrain looked deserted, but for the screams of some exotic birds in a big cage on the very edge of the forest. Stinging nettles had sprung up in the shadow of the trees.

"How much further is it?" asked Delphine.

Andreas pointed to a hill on the horizon.

"We'll be there in fifteen minutes. That's the village over there."

"What is it you want to do here?"

"I haven't been for ten years. My brother still lives there. And probably a couple of my old friends."

"Is it that you want to introduce me to your family?" asked Delphine, and laughed.

The door of the inn opened, and an old woman stepped out. She stopped on the top step and eyed the two newcomers suspiciously. Andreas and Delphine turned around, and returned to the car.

"Shall we go on?" asked Delphine.

Andreas hesitated, then he turned the key.

It was four o'clock when they reached the village. In the industrial zone, which sprawled across the plain, there were a couple of buildings that weren't familiar to Andreas. Other than them, not much seemed to have changed in the last ten years. He was surprised at how well he remembered everything. But there was no emotion accompanying his memory. When he remembered the time of his growing up, it was as though he were leafing in some unknown person's biography, and looking at pictures that weren't anything to do with him.

On a wooden trestle table outside the local foodstore, fireworks were on sale for the upcoming national holiday. Andreas parked behind the hotel, which had been built in the 1970s as part of a convention center. He had worked here as a night porter during his student years. Back then, the building had seemed to him luxurious; now it was small and a bit poky. Inside, it was dark and cool. There was no one at the desk, and it took a long time before anyone answered the bell.

The room smelled of cold cigarette smoke and airfreshener. There was a thick brown carpet on the floor, and multilayered orange curtains in the windows.

Andreas opened the window and looked out. He saw the foot of the hill, the reform church with its bright red roof, and the secondary school where he had gone for three long-forgotten years. He shut the window and drew the curtains. They were so dense that almost no light penetrated the room. Delphine had lain down on the bed, without pulling back the cover. Andreas lay down beside her.

"I can show you round the village, if you like. But it's too hot for that really," he said. "We could go to the swimming pool."

"Is that what you want?"

"I'm sure it'll be full of kids. With weather like this. We always used to go to the lake to swim. There are lots of lakes in the area."

"I'd like to rest for a while," said Delphine.

He kissed her. She said the place had a depressing effect on her already, she couldn't say why. After all, she had hardly seen any of it.

"It's all so perfect here, so spic and span. And everything seems just a little bit small. As if it was built for dwarves."

"The Swiss are taller than the French," said Andreas.

They lay side by side in silence. After a while, Delphine's breathing became deep and regular. She must have fallen asleep.

Andreas thought of summers in his childhood. He pictured himself lying in his parents' garden, reading a book under shady trees. He rode his bike to the river. He jumped from rock to rock in the almost dry river-bed, stumbled, and picked himself up. Then he lay in the tall grass at the edge of the woods up on the hill. He couldn't remember how he had gotten there. A fire was burning almost invisibly, its flames lit and quenched by sunlight. Acrid smoke and the smells and sounds of the forest. Walks, alone or with the family, and always this tiredness and heaviness, that only got better when evening fell. Long evenings outside in a garden restaurant, or once again by the edge of the forest or the side of a lake. Parties that went on until it got cool, and nocturnal rides down the hill on his bike. And then, on the road in front of his parents' house, endless conversations—about love, about life, about everything under the sun. The plans they had made. The world had been so big, then, so full of possibilities.

When Andreas awoke, it was eight o'clock. Delphine was sitting up. She was leaning against the wall, reading a women's magazine she must have brought with her. He asked her if she had been awake a long time.

"I watched you sleep," she said. "I think you were dreaming."

"Something nice?"

"You'd know better than me."

The cigarette machine downstairs was out of his brand. He walked out of the hotel. The air was still heavy and moist. He crossed the market square. The

center of the village was little changed, one or two busi-
nesses had closed, and one or two new ones taken their
place. Where the butcher's shop had been before, there
was now a store that sold tools for the do-it-yourselfer;
the erstwhile dairy was now a children's clothing shop.
There were only a handful of people around, and no one
Andreas knew. The people looked to him like extras in
a film, faceless figures who had taken possession of his
village, pretended they were walking their dogs, looking at shop windows, were on their way home, or to an
evening in the social club. They seemed to feel at home
here, knew their way around, and eyed him curiously
or suspiciously, as though he were the stranger here, not
they.

He looked at the houses, the streets, and the trees
as though somewhere on them would be some traces of
his life here. He saw only silent, apathetic surfaces. He
leaned against one of the old chestnut trees on the market square, rubbed his hand over its dirty gray bark. He
could picture himself walking this way as a child,
going to school, going to music lessons, going home.
The square was empty, and it was very quiet, but the
air seemed somehow animated. Andreas felt strangely
happy, perhaps it was memory, that strange feeling of
happiness that disappeared the second you tried to

focus on it. He tried not to think of anything, but he couldn't manage. A couple of youths came across the square toward him, talking and laughing in loud voices. He pushed off the tree, and walked on to the station. The kiosk there was already shut. He heard a car accelerating away on the other side of the tracks, and then another immediately after. Across the road was a garden restaurant. Andreas went there, passed through the garden into the restaurant. He found a cigarette machine there; it was where he had always gone.

Delphine was sitting on the bed in the room, as though she hadn't moved. She said she had thought he might have abandoned her.

"I would really be in trouble," she said. "I don't even know the name of this place. And I don't speak a word."

They walked around the village, and Andreas pointed out the important places of his childhood, the school, the church where he was confirmed, and the restaurant where he had used to meet his friends. He couldn't imagine what the village looked like to someone seeing it for the first time, and who didn't know its history, and the stories of its inhabitants.

The cemetery was locked. They walked on, crossed the railway line, and reached the swimming baths, and then Andreas's parents' house, where his brother was now living. There was no light on in the windows. They stood at the gate.

"Maybe they're on holiday," suggested Delphine.

"There used to be a place where the key to the basement was hidden," said Andreas. Mechanically, he opened the gate. It squeaked, and Andreas remembered the noise, which hadn't changed from his childhood. He passed through the garden, to the back of the house, and walked down the steps to the basement. Delphine remained at the top. The key was where it always had been, an ancient, rusty thing.

"Come on," whispered Andreas.

It was dark in the basement, there was only one low window through which a little light came in. Andreas remembered the smell right away, a mixture of earth, mold, and heating oil. He took Delphine by the hand, and led her carefully up the steps. The connecting door to the ground floor was not locked. Andreas opened it, and stopped for a moment to listen.

On the kitchen table were a dozen flowerpots, and a little red plastic watering can. Next to it was a sheet of paper with instructions as to which plants needed watering once a week, and which more often.

"They must be on vacation somewhere," he said. "We'd better not turn on any lights. If the neighbors see any, they'll call the police."

"I don't like this. Let's go," said Delphine.

Andreas went into the sitting room. He counted the newspapers piled up on the coffee table, and said presumably they'd be back in the next couple of days. He went out onto the landing, and then up the stairs. Delphine stayed downstairs, and said she didn't want to be arrested. Then she followed him upstairs after all.

The air was warm and stuffy. Andreas's eyes had got used to the darkness, and he found his way around quite easily, though the window shutters were all closed. He stood in his former room, and looked around. The bed and desk were where they had been when they had been his, but the walls were covered with posters of footballers and pop stars who were unfamiliar to him. The room was tidy. Andreas remembered that they had always been made to tidy up before going on holiday. His mother had cleaned the whole house, as though she was afraid she might not come back, and leave dirt and untidiness behind.

Delphine stood next to Andreas.

"Come on," she said. "This is wrong."

"I grew up here," he said. "This is my room."

"It *was* your room, you mean," said Delphine. "Now you've seen it. Can we go?"

"I don't know my brother's children very well," said Andreas.

He had only met his niece and nephew on a couple of occasions. At their grandfather's funeral they had been shy and awkward. And once, a few years ago, the whole family had visited him in Paris. He had booked a hotel for them, and taken them to museums and inexpensive restaurants. But he had mainly spoken to Walter and to Bettina. The children struck him as quiet and polite, but of no interest. They seemed bored when he explained or demonstrated something to them. They looked up at him briefly, and seemed not to hear what he was saying. In restaurants, they only picked dishes they were already familiar with, and they always seemed to be tired, or thirsty, or needing the lavatory. The idea that the family would live on in those individuals, that these were his descendants, his heirs, had always irritated Andreas. And now Maia was eighteen. He knew her age because she was born in the year he moved to Paris. Lukas was three or four years younger.

He should have been more engaged with the children, he thought. It was too late now. He was sure he meant no more to them than they did to him. Their peculiar uncle in Paris, whom their father always talked about with an undertone of anxiety in his voice. If he talked about him at all, that is. Andreas had never been close to his brother. Now he had the feeling of being very close to him, and at the same time, of losing him altogether. He was standing in an empty house.

"It's all gone," he said.

"Come on," said Delphine again, but this time it sounded as though she wanted to comfort him. He followed her slowly down the stairs, and into the open.

It was late when they got back to the hotel. The door was locked, and they had to ring the bell. The night porter was a young man. Andreas asked him what his name was. It was a familiar name, one of his classmates at school had been called that. The young man said he had finished his military service in the spring, and was going to college in the fall. In the meantime he was filling in here. Andreas didn't say anything about his own time as a night porter. It was another hotel, another village, another time.

The next morning they went to the swimming baths. Delphine swam half a mile, and then she leaped from the ten-foot diving board. There was something touching about the way she was showing off in front of Andreas. For the first time, he had a sense of her as younger than himself.

They lay on the river bank, reading. Andreas still felt cool from swimming, the sun that burned his back and legs didn't seem to warm him; only his skin was scorching. For the first time in a while, he felt well. For lunch they bought hotdogs at a stand, and sat down at a wooden table in the shade of some trees.

"What now?" asked Delphine.

"We could go on a trip," said Andreas. "We could go hiking in the mountains, or drive to Lake Constance or to the Rhine Falls."

"But that's not why you came here."

Andreas was silent for a moment. Then he said he had come to the village in the hope of seeing someone.

"A woman?"

"An old girlfriend."

Delphine groaned. "I knew it."

"Knew what?"

"Knew that you'd leave me stranded here, in the middle of nowhere."

"I'm not leaving you stranded. It's ancient history. I've seen her once in twenty years, and that was ten years ago."

"When are you meeting her?"

"I don't even know if she's here at the moment. Maybe she's on vacation as well."

"You drive from Paris to Switzerland to meet her, and you don't even know if she's here?"

Andreas said he would phone Fabienne, he would be back in a moment. He went back to the changing area, and got out his mobile. He called information, and got the number. The idea that he could find himself talking to Fabienne in the next minute made him nervous. He walked rapidly to and fro a couple of times, to the end of the big meadow. He leaned against the wire-mesh fence, and stared out into the forest, which began here. It smelled of earth and mold. When Andreas punched in the number, he wasn't sure that he'd remembered it correctly. Fabienne picked up, using Manuel's family name. Andreas said his name, and there was silence for a moment.

"This is a surprise," said Fabienne, but her voice didn't sound surprised, and Andreas couldn't say whether she was pleased, or whether his calling her was disagreeable to her. "How are you?"

"I'm here."

"What, here in the village?"

"At the baths."

He said he would like to meet her. Did she have time? She said Manuel had taken Dominik to the lake. They would be back around five. Why didn't Andreas come to supper.

"I'm sure Manuel will be pleased."

"I can't make it this evening. Could I see you before that?"

Fabienne hesitated, then she said she was home all day.

"What about three?"

"All right."

Andreas went back to Delphine and said he had arranged to meet Fabienne at three.

"I expect you don't want me at this meeting of yours."

"She's married," said Andreas. "But I don't think it would be very interesting for you. You wouldn't understand anything. And we'll only be talking about old times, anyway."

In the afternoon, more and more children had come into the baths. They played Frisbee and ball and ran around the meadow screeching.

"Shall we go?" said Delphine.

She said she would go and lie down in the hotel for a while. Andreas said if she liked they could go and eat fish together by the lake in the evening. He would book them a table. The restaurant was one they had often gone to for family celebrations.

The afternoon was muggy, and it looked as though a storm was on the way. Andreas walked through a part of the village with single-family homes that had been put up on the other side of the highway. Fabienne had had to tell him the way. When he was a child, it had all been fields and meadows.

The roads in the new subsection were named for wildflowers. Every house was built differently, but they all looked the same, with their white facades and red tiled roofs. Fabienne and Manuel's house was at the end of a cul-de-sac. The garden was enclosed by a picket fence, and looked tidy and well cared for. On the lawn stood a plastic slide and a blue igloo tent.

Even before Andreas had rung the bell, the door opened and Fabienne came out. She was wearing white jeans and a white shirt, and she looked very lovely, fresh and relaxed. Andreas sensed the awkwardness that had always come over her in his presence.

"Our little castle," Fabienne said smiling, and offered Andreas her hand. He took it and kissed her on both cheeks. She invited him in. Would he like a tour of the house? She showed him around from attic to basement and told him about the gas heating and the washing machine. The rooms were not especially distinctive, but it was all nicely done. Other than innumerable family photographs, there were no pictures on the walls. When Fabienne showed him Dominik's room, he asked how old he was.

"He's crazy about water," said Fabienne. "We've got a camper by the lake. In the summer we go there every week, and sometimes on weekday evenings."

"On Manuel's parents' land?"

"It's in the nature reserve," said Fabienne. "You're not allowed to build there, but they allow the camper."

"I've been there with him a couple of times," said Andreas.

In the master bedroom there was a thin foam rubber mat on the floor. Fabienne explained she did exercises. Suddenly she bent down, and did a headstand, stayed on her head for a moment, and then jumped back on her feet. The blood had shot to her head.

From the living room, a sliding door opened on to the terrace. Outside was a white plastic table and chairs, in the shade of a parasol. The table was set.

Fabienne said she had baked a cake, and brewed some ice tea. The cake was still warm. Andreas said she needn't have bothered. She told him to go out, and she would follow.

He sat down on the terrace. The traffic from the highway was only faintly audible, but someone was mowing the lawn on one of the neighboring plots. The smell of freshly cut grass wafted across. Fabienne came out with a tray that had on it an apple cake and a big glass jug of iced tea, with peppermint leaves and ice cubes floating in it. It all might have come out of a housekeeping magazine. She poured a couple of glasses, and sat down opposite Andreas. For a moment they looked at each other in silence. Fabienne smiled, then she looked at the garden, where a lawn sprinkler was moving back and forth.

"Nice you're here," she said. "How do you like my garden?"

She got up, and Andreas followed her over the lawn to a flowerbed, where she showed him some special flowers she'd planted recently. A little further back, she had a couple of plots for vegetables. She said her garden was her empire. Manuel had no interest in it. Unfortunately, it wasn't big enough for everything she had in mind. They strolled back to the table and sat down, and

Fabienne asked what Andreas had been doing with himself all this time.

"What can I say?" he said. "If we'd last seen each other a week ago . . . But now, after so many years."

He said he had worked, eaten, slept, and gone to the cinema. He shrugged. Nothing special.

"I get up early, make coffee, go to work. I lead a regular life. I'm content."

Fabienne asked if he was married, had a family, or a girlfriend. He raised his hands, showed her his bare fingers. He said he had come here with a woman he had recently met, a trainee teacher at his school. But it wasn't anything serious. She was far too young for him. In Paris he had a lover, Sylvie, who was married with three children. Fabienne said nothing. Perhaps she regretted her question. She looked out over the garden, and smiled again, as though she hadn't heard what he had just said. Andreas said that was a nice thing about growing older, that you could take a more relaxed view of these things than when you were, say, twenty. Fabienne didn't take up the subject, and began to talk about people in the village whom Andreas had once known. He had the feeling she was only talking to prevent a silence. She asked him if he remembered Manuel's sister, Beatrice. "She's divorced now. She has three children."

"But she was so religious."

"Not so much now," said Fabienne.

Andreas said he had gone out with Beatrice for a while, but she was so repressed he had left her not much later.

Fabienne said Beatrice had declared one day that she no longer loved her husband. And she didn't want to spend the rest of her life with someone who didn't matter to her. Andreas said that was brave of her. He wouldn't have thought her capable of such a step.

"Everyone thought there was some other man involved. But she lives alone. She seems to be doing fine."

Her brother-in-law often came to talk to Fabienne, but she didn't know what to tell him. No one really knew.

"I don't believe in everlasting love," said Andreas.

For a while Fabienne didn't say anything. She seemed to be thinking. Then she said she and Manuel had been through a couple of rough patches too. Twenty years was a long time. But somehow they had always managed to get back together again. Andreas couldn't imagine strife with Fabienne, raised voices, arguments. He couldn't imagine her depressed, sad, or aggressive.

"For a while, I was doing very badly," she said. "That was ten years ago. I moved out, and went back to my parents in France. Manuel was really sweet to me. He called every day and asked how I was doing, and said Dominik was missing me. I missed them too. After ten days I went back."

"Why?"

Fabienne didn't say anything. She looked at Andreas as though he ought to know, really. Then she got up and went into the garden again. Andreas followed her. The wind had dropped, and the sun was obscured by clouds. The lawn mower had stopped, and it was very quiet. The few sounds you could hear sounded very distinct, as if they were happening nearby, and in an enclosed room. Fabienne had kicked off her slippers, and was walking barefoot on the grass. Andreas saw that she was wearing ankle chains, which didn't go with his idea of her. She turned off the lawn sprinkler and picked up a few garden tools that were left by the flowerbeds. Then she peered over to the edge of the forest, as though she was looking for something.

"Did you see the photos we have in the house?"

Andreas said he had noticed that they didn't have any pictures, just family photos.

"Manuel is a keen amateur photographer," said Fabienne. "He must have taken thousands of pictures. He photographs us all the time. Dominik. Dominik when he's sick. Even when he's asleep."

He had a video camera now, she said. He filmed them all the time. Recently he had begun to copy all his video tapes onto DVDs. Tapes she had never seen before. An uncertain smile. She said sometimes Manuel struck her as very strange, even though she'd known him for such a long time. The uncertain smile again.

"I've never lived with a woman," said Andreas. "I've no idea what that's like."

They went back inside the house. Fabienne put away the garden tools, and asked if Andreas wouldn't have a piece of cake after all. He shook his head, and she seemed to be relieved. She carried the dirty glasses into the kitchen and rinsed them under the tap. Andreas was reminded of detective movies, where the criminals removed all trace of themselves, and ended up forgetting something, like a cigarette butt or a handkerchief.

The light in the hall was dim and yellowish, and the air felt so close that Andreas felt they were underwater. There was a long rumble of thunder outside, echoing away in the distance. Fabienne sat down on a step. Suddenly she looked very tired. Andreas remained standing in front of her, looking down at her. She asked what time it was.

"Half past four."

"Manuel will be back soon."

Andreas sat down beside her. For a moment they sat there in silence, then Fabienne began to speak softly. It was as though she was talking to herself. Her voice sounded mildly amused, as though she didn't take herself seriously, what she was saying, or as if she was talking about somebody else. Sometimes she felt afraid, she said, she didn't know what of.

"It began when Dominik was born. Everything went well. He was an easy child, and not ill very often. Perhaps if I had a reason to feel afraid, it wouldn't be so bad."

On the occasions when Dominik was stung in the mouth by a wasp, when Manuel had fallen down the basement steps and torn a couple of ligaments, she had been afraid too. But she had known what to do, she had provided first aid, she had driven Manuel to the doctor. The fear she really had in mind was much more diffuse, a feeling of strangeness, of not belonging. Manuel and Dominik sometimes appeared really strange to her. When they were down in the basement tinkering with something, or when they went out fishing together, she had these strange notions about what they were all doing. The life they were living, this house they had built, the photographs on the walls. Sometimes she imagined the house burning down, or some other disaster, and these imaginings had a somehow liberating effect on her. Andreas asked her if she ever talked about it with Manuel. She shook her head and stood up. "What would I say to him?"

Andreas said he had brought her something. He took the book out of his pocket, and passed it to her.

"What is it?"

"A little book. Do you know the author?"

"Never heard of him."

"Read it," said Andreas. "It might remind you of something."

"How long are you staying in the village?"

"I'll be here for a while. I'll call you."

The storm hadn't begun yet. The clouds had pushed past, only in the east was the sky still dark, as though night had begun to fall. It was five o'clock when Andreas got back to the hotel. Delphine wasn't there, and she hadn't left him a message either. He called her on her mobile, but only got put through to her mailbox. He waited for her in the room. At seven she still wasn't there. He turned on the TV. An early evening series was on, and Andreas tried for a time to follow it, but the characters all looked too alike, and he soon lost track of what was happening.

A little after half past seven Delphine walked in. Her hair was wet, and she was carrying a plastic bag under her arm. Andreas was furious. He asked her where she'd been, and why she hadn't left a message. She said she hadn't known when she'd be back. He could hardly expect her to sit in the room all afternoon.

"You could at least have left your cell phone switched on."

"It doesn't work abroad."

Again Andreas asked her where she'd been. She said she'd gone for a walk. In a garden restaurant she had gotten into conversation with a group of young people. One of them was the night porter here at the hotel. She had asked him what there was to do here. He said there wasn't anything.

"They asked me where I'm from, and what I'm doing here, and we talked for a bit."

The young people said they were going for a swim in the lake, and did Delphine fancy coming with them.

"You mean to say you went swimming with a bunch of total strangers?"

"It's not so bad. They were really friendly. Their French isn't up to much, but somehow we managed to make ourselves understood."

"Our table's booked for half past seven. It takes half an hour to get to the Untersee."

Delphine said she'd agreed to go to a barbecue with the young people. She had only gone back to the hotel to fetch him. He had told her he was booking a table, said Andreas. He didn't want to have a barbecue with a load of total strangers.

"Don't be a spoilsport," said Delphine. "I spent all day doing what you wanted."

The young people were parked in front of the hotel. There were three men and two women, and all of them seemed to be younger than Delphine. All evening Andreas was unable to establish who was going out with whom, or if they were all just good friends. He asked the night porter whether he wasn't working. He shook his head and said not until tomorrow. One of the men had completed a business studies course, the other one seemed not to be doing anything. One of the women was still at school, and another was helping out in her parents' bakery. They shook hands with Andreas, and made room for him and Delphine in one of the two cars.

"Where are we going?" asked the night porter, who was driving.

"To the Dreispitz. That's a place on the river."

Andreas said he knew; he had been there himself many times.

At the sewage plant, they had to leave the cars, and do the last part on foot, through the forest, and over the dam and across an unmown meadow full of molehills. The fire site was at the very end of the meadow in a sandy hollow, where the canal joined the river at an acute angle. The young men had collected wood in the forest, and one of them lit a fire.

The river had been straightened a long time ago, and its banks were reinforced with untrimmed blocks of stone. Andreas scrambled down to the water. He sat on a stone, and lit a cigarette. The conversations of the others were boring. With their lousy French, they were asking Delphine what music she liked, her favorite films, her plans for the future. They made jokes about her name. They drank beer and ate sausages they grilled over the fire.

Gradually it got dark. One of the guys had brought a portable CD player, and put on music that Andreas didn't know, and that he thought was dreadful. He felt old and out of place, and hardly spoke all evening. It got a bit chilly. He hoped they would all go home soon.

Finally, at midnight they packed everything away. The fire was not quite out, and one of the men said, OK, guys, do your duty, and he unzipped his pants. The others did the same, and all three of them stood around the fire. The women took a couple of steps back. The embers hissed, and the smell of piss spread through the air. The baker's daughter said they were revolting, and the other woman laughed, as did Delphine. She shot Andreas a triumphant look.

It was pitch-black in the forest. The night porter had a flashlight with him, and went on ahead. Delphine took Andreas's hand. When they reached the cars, one of the women said they were going dancing in a discotheque in the next village. She asked Delphine and Andreas if they wanted to come. Andreas said he was tired.

"I'd better put this old man to bed," said Delphine, and the others laughed. Presumably they found Andreas just as boring as he found them.

"The night porter was staring at you the whole time," said Andreas, once he was lying in bed with Delphine.

"Did you think?"

"It made me wonder if I was like that when I was their age."

"Are you starting that again."

Andreas said he was only wondering what she saw in such company.

"Well, if you don't see it, then you just don't see it, I suppose."

Over the next few days, they went on a couple of side trips. One day, they went to the lake where Andreas had kissed Fabienne. Everything looked just as it had then, only there were some cigarette butts in the grass and empty plastic bottles. They had the place to themselves. They swam a bit, and then lay in the sun to dry. They walked around the lake, and then into the forest, until they came to a little hollow.

"Just like a bed," said Andreas.

They took off their clothes and made love on the dry leaves. Andreas closed his eyes and tried to imagine he was with Fabienne, but he couldn't do it. The ground was hard, and Delphine said there was something sticking in her back, and Andreas ought to try lying underneath. Then they swam some more. When the sun disappeared behind the trees, they packed their things and drove back to the village.

On the national holiday, they climbed up onto the hill and watched the fire. The inhabitants of the village stood in a large circle around the wooden pyre. The children were setting off fireworks. Their faces glowed in the sheen of the flames. After a while Andreas pulled Delphine out of the circle, and they strolled along the ridge. Down in the valley and on hills opposite, they saw the fires of the other villages, and from time to time they saw the little detonations of fireworks that looked tiny in the distance. The moon was full, and the landscape was in plain view, the village, the road, the cars, and, once, a short train, heading for the village, and disappearing between its houses.

"It looks like a toy landscape," said Delphine. "Little people driving in little cars. Little houses, a little church, you see, it's all there."

Andreas said he sometimes wondered what his life would have been like if he had never left the village.

"Then I wouldn't be here," said Delphine. "You'd never have met me."

Maybe I wouldn't have got sick, Andreas thought, or not so suddenly. He would have slowly grown older, would have fallen in love, married, had children. He would be here for the national holiday with his whole family, slowly they would climb the hill, saying hello left and right. Then the children would light the fireworks they would have brought with them. Andreas told them to be careful. He would be standing beside his wife with the other grownups, watching the children, who were now chasing around the fire, throwing in boughs they had gotten from the forest. At his back he felt the chill of night, in his face the heat of the fire. Then they would all go home. In the house it would be oppressively warm, and the light would dazzle him. He sat down on the hallway steps, and took his shoes off. Then he would lie down beside his wife. The window shutters would be closed, but the window would be open. He lay awake and listened to the night outside. From the neighbors' gardens would come the sound of laughter and the jingle of glasses. and from further afield the bang of a firework, and shortly afterward the barking of a dog who couldn't settle.

"Let's go," said Delphine, "I'm cold."

The next day they went swimming again. Then the weather took a final turn for the worse. It was sultry all day long. Finally, late in the afternoon, the storm broke. Andreas and Delphine were sitting in the garden restaurant eating ice cream, as the sky turned black in a matter of minutes, and violent gusts tugged at the umbrellas. They barely had time to pack their things and take shelter under the roof before the rain broke loose. When the storm was over, they saw clouds of steam rising off the asphalt road. The next day, it rained all day.

Andreas was woken by Delphine. He watched her for a while. He pushed up her nightie. As he tried to take her panties off, she half woke, and, without saying a word, helped him. It was close in the room, and Delphine was wet with night sweat, and somehow cool. She had only briefly opened her eyes, and quickly shut them again. She was smiling, bit her lip, threw her head back, and turned it to the side. Little beads of sweat formed on her upper lip; Andreas kissed them away. Her face grew serious, looked strained, concentrated, for a moment she seemed to be in pain, then she relaxed again.

"*Tu es gentil,*" she said, and her eyes opened. "What's that in German?"

"Friendly," said Andreas, "kind, nice."

"Nice," repeated Delphine. She got up and went to the bathroom. She came back and got straight into her underwear.

They only just made it down to breakfast in time. Then they went back upstairs. Andreas read the newspaper, Delphine rummaged around in the bathroom, painted her toenails, and plucked her eyebrows. It was almost noon. Andreas opened the window and looked outside at the rain falling on the parking lot. The air had cooled down, and there was a smell of wet asphalt. Delphine came out of the bathroom, and leaned out of the window beside him.

"The forecast is poor," he said. "It's supposed to rain solidly for the next few days."

"How much longer do you want to stay here?"

Andreas hesitated for a moment, then he said he felt good here, everything was familiar, the landscape, the climate, the names of the plants. Here, he said, he knew what was coming. Delphine countered that he had spent more of his adult life in Paris than in Switzerland.

"But this is where I grew up," said Andreas. "I feel I never really arrived in Paris."

He said his walk to school went around a large field. When the ground was frozen in winter, he would take a shortcut across the field. One time, it was the morning of Christmas Eve. It was still dark, and there was fog over the field.

"The teacher asked us to bring candles. In the middle of the field, I came to a stop. Over by the highway, the fog was dyed orange by the streetlights. I knelt down and pushed my candle into the earth and lit it.

Don't ask me why. I knelt down on the frozen ground, and watched it burn down. And then I went on to school."

"Children are peculiar," said Delphine. But she didn't understand why he was telling her this. Andreas said he wasn't going back to Paris.

"How do you mean?"

"I've given my notice."

"Are you crazy?" Delphine looked at him in horror. "What's gotten into you?"

Andreas didn't reply. There was nothing he could have said. A truck drove up, and a man got out, and began to unload crates of bottles.

"What do you want to do here? Work as a German teacher?"

Andreas said he had enough money.

"Is it that woman?"

"I don't think so," said Andreas.

When he turned toward Delphine, he saw she was crying. He put his arm around her, and held her close. She broke away, and they stood silently side by side, watching the delivery man at work.

"If you need money for the train," said Andreas.

Delphine looked at him, and shook her head.

They went to the station, and Delphine bought a

ticket and reserved a berth. The train didn't leave until ten, they had a lot of time. They drove up the hill to a restaurant with a view of the village, and down to the valley. From there you could see the river, and the wooded slopes and the mountains on the horizon. You could hear the traffic all the way from the highway. It had stopped raining, but the sky was still cloudy. Only in the west was there a little patch of brightness. The low sun made the clouds look darker.

It was cold out on the terrace, and the tables and chairs were wet with rain. Andreas and Delphine sat inside, at a table by a window. The place was almost empty. The landlady came. Andreas remembered her from before, she was only a few years older than him, and she had been a pretty girl then. Now she was a heavyset woman with a tired face. She seemed not to recognize him, and he didn't say he was local.

Delphine had ordered a salad, but she hardly touched it, and pushed it away after a little while. Andreas wasn't hungry either. He said it was a pity she was going already.

"What would have been the point of staying?" said Delphine, and she started crying again. The landlady came. She didn't let on, only asked whether they were done, and if everything had been all right.

He just wasn't cut out for steady relationships, said Andreas, after the landlady had gone.

"That's not even the point," said Delphine. "Do you think I want to marry you?"

"So what is the point, then?"

"I don't know what to say to you," said Delphine, half crying, half laughing. "If you don't know that, then I can't help you either."

She could tell his mind was on this other women, she said. Andreas angrily shook his head.

"Nonsense," he said. "She's happily married."

"That's your problem."

They were at the station far too early. Andreas parked the car on the other side of the road, in front of the post office. Old chestnut trees surrounded the parking lot, giving a dense canopy of leaves, and keeping away the light of the streetlamps.

Andreas got Delphine's suitcase out of the trunk. She took it from him and said she was going to say good-bye to him here. She didn't want a scene on the platform. She embraced him and kissed him on the lips and went away without another word. She crossed the road, and disappeared around the corner of the station building. Andreas waited in the car until the train had pulled in and left again. He had the radio tuned to a classical station, and remembered the train they had seen three days before from the top of the hill, the toy train running through the toy landscape.

He had opened the side window a bit, and cool air flowed in. He asked himself if it was true that he really wasn't made for long relationships. It was what he had always told himself. Maybe he just hadn't met the right woman. Perhaps Fabienne would have been right for him—or Delphine was.

He drove to the part of the village where Fabienne lived. He parked by the side of the road, and went on on foot. A white camper was parked outside Fabienne's house. The windows facing the street were curtained off. There wasn't much to see from the pavement, just that the light was still on in the kitchen. Andreas pictured Manuel and Fabienne sitting in the kitchen, drinking a glass of wine together. He imagined Manuel having a headache, and getting up to take a painkiller. Fabienne woke up and followed him. She asked him what the matter was, and Manuel said it was nothing, he was coming straight back to bed. She stayed in the doorway for a moment. Then she went to the toilet, half-numb with tiredness, went back to bed, and fell asleep. The light in the kitchen went out.

Andreas felt very tired. He stood outside the house, staring at the dark windows. When a woman with a dog passed along the street, he walked on. Their paths crossed. The dog barked, and the woman pulled at the leash and told it off.

The next day the sky was still cloudy, and a cool wind blew. When Andreas put his jacket on, the letter that had been in his mailbox on his last morning in the apartment dropped into his hand. It was from Nadia. Andreas couldn't recall ever having seen her handwriting before, which was big and a little wild and hard to decipher.

The letter was several pages long. Once again, the subject was emptiness, neglect, and the lack of love. She had tried, wrote Nadia, to make up for the shortage of love in her life with sex. Following her separation from her husband, she had embarked on a rather wild phase, in which she had gone with men pretty casually. It was at that time that they had met. Perhaps she had misused him for her own ends, as he had misused her for his. But she had felt empty from the very beginning. In the meantime, she had got back together with her ex-husband, and they were going to try a fresh start together. She wrote to say that she hoped he would be happy, and that—and then there were some words that he couldn't read—and that he too would feel the peace that she now felt.

Andreas put the last page of the letter on the table with the others. He was glad there were no hard feelings from Nadia. It had never occurred to him that she was exploiting him. That idea fascinated him. He knew people could ask for anything from him. He would do whatever was required, and if he noticed he was being taken advantage of, then at the most he would be angry with himself. Everything would be much easier if you could see yourself as a victim, he thought, a victim of your childhood, of fate, of the people you had grown up among, and finally too, as a victim of illness. But in order to feel himself a victim, he had to believe in the possibility of another, better life. Andreas believed in nothing but chance. He loved the curious coincidences and repetitions that life threw up, against all logic. He loved the surprising patterns that came about in the sky, or on a body of water or in the shade of a tree, the continual tiny adjustments in the same overall context. Nadia called it nihilism; his own word for it was modesty.

After breakfast, he called Fabienne. She asked if he wanted to speak to Manuel, who was down in the basement.

"Did you tell him you saw me?"

There was quiet for a moment, then Fabienne said, no, she hadn't, she wasn't sure if he would have wanted that.

"Can we see each other?"

"Manuel and Dominik are building a hot-air balloon. I don't know if they're going out today or not. Maybe if the wind drops, they will."

"Can you get away?"

"I'll have to be back here at twelve by the latest."

She thought about it. Then she said they could meet by the camper. Would he remember the way? She said she'd be waiting for him in the parking lot in half an hour.

As Andreas drove down the narrow gravel track, he saw Fabienne's white camper in the empty parking lot. He was a bit late, but he hadn't been here for twenty years, and had taken a wrong turning and gotten briefly lost. He parked next to Fabienne, and for a moment they looked at each other, as if they had happened to stop together at a traffic light or in a department store parking garage. Andreas got out, and walked around the car.

He could hear music softly playing. Fabienne leaned forward, and the music stopped. She climbed out and kissed him on both cheeks. She was wearing jeans and a yellow slicker.

"You're prepared for anything, aren't you," he said. As for himself, he had his swimming trunks with him.

"It's supposed to rain again in the afternoon," said Fabienne.

Even though she had already told him on the phone, he asked her again how much time she had. She said she would have to go back at half past eleven at the latest. She asked him what he had done in the past few days. She unlocked the gate, and locked it again after them. If she ever forgot to lock it, she said, people would be in there in no time, lighting fires and leaving their trash lying around.

They stood in a big meadow with old trees. To either side of them, the land was bordered by wild hedges, and on the lake side by a wide growth of rushes. A wooden boardwalk led through the rushes to the water.

They strolled over the meadow, as though aimlessly, just to stretch their legs. Fabienne bent to pick up some toys in the grass, and put them away in the camper.

"Do you think the season's over for this year?" asked Andreas.

"We often come here in the autumn too," said Fabienne. "Even in winter. We have a little rowboat. Manuel and Dominik go fishing in it."

The sun shone in between the clouds, and everything glistened in its light. There was an almost transparent haze in the trees and the reeds. Andreas and Fabienne walked along the boardwalk through the rushes. At the end of it, they sat down on the wooden planking, and looked out across the lake. The air was very clear, and the German shore seemed almost within reach.

"Look," said Fabienne, pointing to a crested grebe, diving not far from where they were. They waited in silence until it emerged on the surface again. Andreas lay down on his belly and dipped his hand in the water.

"The water's warmer than the air," he said. "Do you fancy a swim?"

"Why not," said Fabienne. "Seeing as we're here."

She got changed in the camper, he outside in the meadow. She appeared in the doorway and took his bundle of clothes from him, and put it in the camper.

He walked across the meadow after her. She was walking faster than a moment ago, perhaps she was cold, or she sensed his eyes on her. She was wearing a one-piece bathing suit and had tied a scarf around her waist. Andreas tried to remember what she had looked like when he had first met her. Ever since he had seen her again, his old images of her were rubbed out. He had told her she hadn't changed, but she must have in all that time.

The water was colder than he'd expected. The chill took his breath away. They swam a little way out into the lake, and then parallel to the shore. Andreas had overtaken Fabienne, and was swimming on ahead in short strokes, so as not to pull away from her. After a few hundred yards, they turned and swam back.

Andreas climbed out of the water. Fabienne held on to the metal ladder, and did some leg kicks. She looked up at him and smiled. He paced up and down the pier, shaking his arms, and once or twice jumping up and down. Then Fabienne too came out. They wrapped themselves in their towels, and sat side by side on the pier, so close that their shoulders touched. The sun was gone. Andreas was gibbering with cold.

"Aren't you cold?" he asked.

"A little bit."

For a while they looked out across the lake in silence, then Andreas laid his hand on Fabienne's shoulder.

Suddenly he felt very young and unsure of himself. He cleared his throat.

"Yes?" said Fabienne, and Andreas asked her if she remembered how he had kissed her twenty years before. She said it hadn't been so cold that day. He said he had loved her very much back then.

He looked at her from the side, her profile, her slender neck and shoulders, on which a few drops of water glistened, the hair, darker at the ends. She looked out at the lake, and said in a slightly throaty voice that she hadn't been aware of anything.

"I wrote you a letter. But I never mailed it."

"You're freezing," said Fabienne. "Come on, let's get dressed."

They ran along the boardwalk, and through the damp grass to the camper. Andreas got out of breath and started coughing. He followed Fabienne into the camper. She passed him his things. He was still hesitating while Fabienne peeled off her suit and hung it on a clothesline that already had a boy's trunks on it. For a moment she stood naked in front of him. She smiled, half uncertain, half provocative, then she turned her back to him and got dressed.

They left the place. Andreas looked at his watch, it wasn't ten yet. In silence they walked along a path, away from the parking lot, past a couple of fenced-in estates, and a large meadow. The path was winding back toward the lake, but the water couldn't be seen for the reeds. After a few hundred yards, the path divided, and one half led into the reed bed. Fabienne went ahead, Andreas followed. The path ended in a wooden observation platform. They climbed up the ladder-like steps. On top was a sign that said the platform had been built by the birdwatchers' association, "for bird-lovers everywhere, who have not lost the capacity for wonder."

Fabienne leaned over the handrail, and looked out at the lake. She asked if Andreas was still feeling cold. No, he said, it was better now. He was standing just behind her. He grasped her shoulders with both hands. She lowered her head, and leaned forward a little. He held her hips, and pushed his hands under her waterproof jacket. She stood up a little straighter, otherwise she barely moved. He kissed her neck, stroked her breasts. She turned around. When he tried to kiss her mouth, she turned her face away. He tried to shove his hand in her jeans. She broke away, and undid her belt and top button.

"It's easier like this," she said.

They made love on the observation platform. The boards were wet and cold. Fabienne took off her jeans and shoes. She pushed up her sweatshirt and her bra, but left on her jacket. She kept her eyes shut, and lay there motionless. She seemed very naked and vulnerable. Andreas was put in mind of police photographs of crime scenes, pale, lifeless bodies by the side of the road, in forests or rushes.

They said good-bye at the parking lot. Andreas got in his car and watched Fabienne put on her seat belt, get into reverse, and drive off. She seemed perfectly calm, as though nothing had happened. Andreas put on his seat belt, but didn't drive away. It had begun to drizzle, and the landscape was half-obscured from sight. It was cold in the car, and Andreas's breath made clouds of steam. He thought about Fabienne. He was surprised by the purposefulness with which she had guided his hands, the calmness of her surrender, and her sudden quick pleasure. The whole thing was over in fifteen minutes. Then Fabienne had got a packet of Kleenex out of her jacket, and carefully wiped herself. She seemed very strange to Andreas. It was as though her face had also changed from being naked. He didn't recognize her until she was dressed again.

He didn't know what he expected from her. He didn't even know what he wanted. That she leave her family for him? That she go with him to France, or wherever? That she become his mistress, meet him every other week somewhere, always with a guilty conscience where she was concerned? They would get used to each other, maybe even quicker than two spouses got used to each other, because they wouldn't share anything but their love.

He hadn't returned to the village to start a relationship, but to end one, to have certainty at last. If Fabienne had slapped him when he tried to kiss her, either back then or today, he would have gotten over it, as he had gotten over other unhappy relationships. He was concerned to get an answer from her, to know at last whether she loved him, whether she might have been able to love him. But in fact she hadn't given him an answer. She told him not to call her at home. He asked her how else was he going to get ahold of her. She said she would call him tomorrow.

He ate in the fish restaurant where he had wanted to take Delphine. Earlier, it had been renowned for its good cooking, but he didn't enjoy the food. It would be nice if Delphine were here, he thought.

He stayed up in his room all afternoon. He hoped Fabienne would call. Suddenly he wasn't sure whether he had given her the correct room number. Maybe she had forgotten the number, and she was calling reception, and no one was answering.

Fabienne called the next morning, as she had said she would.

"Can we meet up?"

"Manuel and Dominik are flying their hot-air balloon," she said. "I'm free till twelve."

"Do you want to meet at the camper?"

"They've taken the car."

They arranged to meet at the hut in the woods where they had first met.

Andreas walked through the village, and through the business district. The sky was clear, except for some little shreds of cirrus clouds. The forecast was for warm weather in the afternoon, but the morning felt cool. It was the first day of autumn, the sky looked suddenly darker, and the air was so clear that everything seemed very close.

Andreas got to the rendezvous too early. There were wet charred branches on the campfire site, and garbage on the ground. The hut belonged to the community, and on the wall, in a little metal frame, was a list of rules. Andreas perused it: garbage in the containers provided, no loud music, no dogs without a leash.

Fabienne came almost exactly on time. Once again, she was wearing the yellow slicker. She propped her bike against a tree. Andreas hugged her, she kissed him on both cheeks.

"Do you want to go for a walk?"

They walked through the forest. It was probably the same path they had taken that night when they played hide and seek. It led on and on in a straight line. In the distance you could see where the forest ended. For a while they walked in silence side by side. Then Fabienne asked Andreas what was in the letter that he had written but not sent.

"That I love you," said Andreas. "Not much more than that, I think."

He asked what she would have done if she'd received the letter.

"I don't know," said Fabienne. She seemed to be thinking. She said she was really fond of Manuel. They had a good relationship.

"When did it begin, with the two of you?"

"I suppose it was the day you kissed me. He was very attentive. He took me home. I was a bit confused."

"Ah, if I'd had the car."

"But nothing happened," said Fabienne. "We just talked. You were so dismissive, after you'd kissed me. You behaved as though it was nothing. And then you got really aggressive. I told Manuel about your kissing me. We talked about you a long time. That brought us closer. The next day he brought me flowers. We didn't kiss until much later."

Andreas said he didn't suppose he'd ever loved a woman as much as he'd loved her. Fabienne didn't say anything. They walked slowly through the forest, side by side. Andreas was a little surprised he didn't feel angry with Manuel, that he didn't even feel jealous of him. He wouldn't have wanted to trade places with him. He stopped and pressed Fabienne to himself. He kissed her on the mouth, but she didn't reciprocate. She hugged him like a good friend, and laid her head against his chest.

"There's no point," she said.

"One night," he said. "Let's spend one night together. To give us something to remember. Not just those ten minutes."

"Love lasts for ten minutes," said Fabienne. "What difference would it make?"

"What made you sleep with me, anyway?"

"I was curious," said Fabienne, and then, a while later, she couldn't just stay away from home for a night, she didn't know what he was thinking of. In the fifteen years she'd been married to Manuel, she had spent very few nights away from him.

"Do you remember our meetings in Paris?"

"I just remember the fact of them," said Fabienne, with an apologetic smile.

"In the mosque," said Andreas. "And one time we went to the cinema. The film tore, and they were unable to show us the ending. Someone came up to the front and told us the ending."

"I don't remember."

It was all so long ago, said Fabienne. So much had happened in the meantime.

"Not in my life," said Andreas.

They had gotten to the edge of the forest, and stopped. The path led on, past the gravel pit, and through fields and meadows to the next village.

"Are you happy?" asked Andreas.

"I'm not unhappy," said Fabienne. "Let's go back."

Andreas said he had the feeling of having done something incredibly stupid that would never be made up for.

"I can still remember writing the letter. I had something to eat in a pizza place near the Opera. It was evening, I was alone, and I started writing in my notebook, about our first meeting, and driving to the lake, and kissing you. Our story. And that I wanted it to continue. If I'd had an envelope and a stamp, I think I might have mailed it to you right away. But the next morning, I no longer dared."

They were silent. Andreas wondered if the relationship could have lasted. They had both been so young. Maybe he would have made Fabienne unhappy, maybe they would have split up long ago. Or they would still be together, one of those couples that stick together because they're each so afraid of being alone. They didn't really fit. At that time, it hadn't seemed to matter to him. He wanted to convince himself that the only reason his love had lasted so long was because it had remained unrequited. He asked Fabienne what she was thinking. Nothing, she said.

"What does your girlfriend say about you going to meet me all the time?"

"That's over. She went back to France. It wasn't anything serious."

"Tell me about her."

Andreas said he didn't know what to say about Delphine. He didn't want to think about her or talk about her, least of all with Fabienne.

"What does she look like?"

"Short brown hair, quite a pretty face. About as tall as you, but not such a beautiful figure."

"How old is she?"

"Twenty-four."

"Do you love her?"

"I don't think so. Certainly not as much as I loved you."

As I love you, he thought, but didn't say it. He said there had been a time that he could imagine starting a family, having children, settling down somewhere. But that time had passed. He couldn't even claim to regret it. He wasn't sure he still wanted to love someone as passionately as when he was twenty.

"What about her? Does she love you?"

"I don't know. I think she might."

"And isn't that enough for you?"

She asked what had made Delphine go back.

Andreas wanted to tell her that he wasn't going back to Paris, that he would stay in the village, but suddenly his plan struck him as absurd. He had come here on her account. If the story with her was over, there was no sense in staying here. He said he had quarreled with Delphine. Something trivial.

"That's none of my business," said Fabienne.

They were back at the hut. Fabienne said she was expected at home, her menfolk would be back soon.

"And you're making lunch for them."

"Yes," said Fabienne. "I'm making lunch for them."

"Will you tell Manuel? About what happened?"

Fabienne shook her head. What for? She gave Andreas her hand and said good-bye. He shook hands, and kissed her on the cheeks. She got on her bike. She had ridden a few yards when she stopped.

"I almost forgot something," she said. She got down, and pulled the little book Andreas had given her out of her jacket pocket. He came a little nearer, but he didn't take the book.

"Did you read it?"

"Yes."

"And?"

"There must be hundreds of stories like ours."

"But all the details. The fact that I called you Butterfly . . ."

"That wasn't you. That was Manuel's name for me."

"And the cat she buys herself when she returns to Paris?"

"I never had a cat."

Andreas asked if she was sure. Fabienne laughed at him.

"That must have been a different girl."

"I suppose it's the story of you and Manuel, then," said Andreas.

"No," said Fabienne, "it is our story. What I have with Manuel isn't a story. It's reality."

They stood and faced each other. Then Fabienne put her arms around Andreas and kissed him on the mouth. It was their first kiss. Her lips were dry and a little rough, it was the kiss of a young girl. They kissed for a long time until they were both out of breath.

"Keep the book," said Andreas as they finally broke.

Fabienne smiled. Without another word, she got on her bike and rode off. Andreas watched her go. She stood on the pedals, the bicycle swayed from side to side. The road led along the edge of the forest, past a meadow full of old fruit trees and a farmhouse. By the time Fabienne reached the first houses in the village, she was just a yellow dot.

Andreas went back to the hut, and sat down on the wooden bench that ran along the front of it. He felt weak, but his head was clearer than it had been for months. He felt nothing but a kind of jaunty indifference. It was as though he had got rid of a weight, something that had been oppressing him for eighteen years. Presumably his life would have been different if he had mailed the letter then. There was even something mildly consoling about that. If Fabienne had turned him down then, his long wait would have seemed even more pointless.

He tried to remember time spent with her, but he kept coming back to the same scenes. The forest, the lake, the cinema in Paris. He remembered every particular, saw Manuel, Beatrice, the other young men and women they hung around with that summer, he even saw himself. Only Fabienne looked oddly out of focus in those scenes. But with that last kiss—their first kiss— Fabienne had finally come to life. It was only the kiss that counted.

Andreas thought about his childhood, his growing up, the time when happiness or misery, love or panic had been able to fill him completely. When time itself seemed to stand still, and there was no way out. He no longer wanted to love the way he had at twenty, but sometimes he missed the intensity of feeling he had had at that age. And those moments, in which everything suddenly was over, that feeling of total insignificance, and at the same time of complete freedom. A pure perspective on the world that almost took his breath away with its beauty, the patterning on a piece of wood, some peeling paint, a little shred of paper left under a thumbtack, the rust stain on the head of a nail. He ran his hand over the bench he was sitting on, over the wall of blackened, weathered boards he was leaning against. He inhaled deeply, and smelled the damp and moldy smell of the forest, and the sweet accent of some late-flowering bush. He could remember how he had felt, but he couldn't feel like that anymore.

He probably wouldn't see Fabienne again. Anyway, it didn't matter if he did or not. Their story was at an end. One story among a very great many that began and ended at each moment.

Andreas walked along the road toward the village. He passed the little general store where he had sometimes bought candy when he was a boy. He came by here on his way to school, and when he had money he would go in and buy chocolate or biscuits. Back then, he had always been hungry, and had always eaten a lot of sweets between meals. Over the years, his appetite had decreased. Some days, he didn't eat much more than a sandwich at lunch, and another one at night.

He walked into the store, and went up and down the aisles. He bought a bottle of wine, and a couple of bars of chocolate. There was a young woman sitting at the cash register. To go by her accent, she wasn't from around here. She made some comment about the weather. It had been a bad summer, she said, and Andreas nodded and said one could only hope that the fall would be nicer.

"Maybe it'll warm up again."

The checkout girl said she doubted it.

Andreas walked down the street where he had grown up. It was midday, and there was no one out in any of the gardens. One house had got a new coat of paint, another had had a garage built on to it. Apart from that, nothing seemed to have changed. The enormous pine opposite Andreas's parents' house had been cut down. Where it had once stood, there was now only a stump, and, beside it, a newly planted sapling. It will take decades to grow as tall as the old tree, thought

Andreas. It wouldn't happen in his lifetime, or his brother's or Bettina's—maybe not even the children would get to see that happen.

As Andreas stepped through the squeaky gate, Walter appeared at the open window. He looked at Andreas in bewilderment.

"What are you doing here?" he called out.

The next moment he came running down the garden path, then stopped. He seemed to hesitate. Andreas also hesitated, then he put his arms around his brother. Clumsily, Walter did likewise.

"Come in," he said. "We were just about to have lunch."

Andreas handed over the bottle.

"A Bordeaux," said Walter, looking at the bottle appraisingly.

Andreas said he just wanted to look over the house and take a peek at the garden.

The flowerbeds were choked with a low growth of weeds, and the hazel bush on the west side had spread, and was now almost as high as the roof. Walter said the garden was his responsibility, but he didn't have enough time. He was glad if he got around to mowing the grass every other week. Things grew pretty much as they pleased.

As they walked into the house, Bettina was just setting a fifth place. She must have seen the visitor through the window. She too seemed to be so happy about his presence that Andreas felt a little embarrassed. She hugged him. Maia had grown into a pretty girl. She was taller than Bettina, and had a confident air about her. Lukas was a couple of heads shorter, a quiet boy, who reminded Andreas of his brother. He gave them each a bar of chocolate, and said he hoped they weren't too old for such things. Maia laughed and said you were never too old for chocolate.

Over lunch, they talked about people from the village. Walter said next door's pine had been struck by lightning, and had had to be cut down. Some of the houses were now occupied by the children that had gone to school with him and Andreas. The two old sisters in the corner house had moved into the assisted-living center long ago. One of them had died since, said Bettina. Walter said that was news to him.

"But I told you," said Bettina. "I went to the funeral. It must be a year ago now."

"What about their shop?"

"It was sold. It belongs to a chain now. But it's not doing any better than before."

At the edge of the village, a shopping center had been built, Walter explained. The small local shops had trouble competing. There was one butcher shop left in the village. They counted the number of butcher shops there had once been, and they got to seven.

After lunch, the children grabbed their chocolate, and ran upstairs to their rooms. Walter called work to take the afternoon off. The conversation took a while, there was something he needed to explain to a colleague. Bettina put on water for coffee. She leaned against the stove, and said their living there now must feel strange to him.

"If I know Walter, you won't have changed many things."

Bettina laughed, and then she was serious again. She said the death of their father had affected Walter very badly.

"If at least he'd talked about it. But he didn't say anything, not one word. He continued to function, like a machine. At first, when we moved in here, it was terrible. You couldn't change a thing, not take a picture off the walls, nothing. He made us put all our things down in the basement. If I moved a piece of furniture, in the evening he would move it back to its old place, and not say a word. It was back and forth. Eventually, he gave up, and let me do some of what I wanted. But if it had been up to him, everything would still look exactly the way it did then."

"The garden reminded me of before," said Andreas. "Even though it was never as neglected as it is now."

He said they had been through a lot, living in this house, but he couldn't see it with the same eyes as then.

"Everything's still there, I remember every detail. But it doesn't have the same importance anymore."

"There are still a couple of boxes of yours upstairs," said Bettina. "School things, I think. Books and toys."

Andreas said they could throw them away.

"Don't you even want to look at them?"

"I looked through some old notes not long ago. It was weird. At times it felt as though I'd written them the day before, at times it was like someone from another planet. And I have to say neither kind was at all interesting."

Bettina said she would hang on to the things. Maybe he would change his mind. There was enough room. Andreas asked after the children. Maia was taking her final exams next spring, said Bettina. She was very good at math. With Lukas, she didn't know yet. He was just starting high school. There was plenty of time to decide. He was a dreamy boy, she said, like a child in many ways. He reminded her of Andreas.

"Of me?"

"That's what Walter says too. Didn't you see the similarity? He has your eyes. Your father's eyes."

They drank coffee in the garden. Walter asked how Andreas was feeling, and he said he had a persistent cough, but he thought he was getting over it. Apart from that, everything was fine.

"Do you still smoke as much?" asked Bettina.

"I'll stop at some point."

"That's what they all say."

Andreas said he'd rather talk about something else. Walter asked if he wanted to see their parents' grave. Yes, said Andreas, why not. When Walter went into the house to get his jacket, Bettina asked about Andreas's cough. He said he had had to take a couple of tests, but had left before the results came through.

"You're worried."

"Yes," said Andreas. "I'm worried."

"It doesn't change it whether you know it or not. But you don't need me to tell you that."

"I just wanted to take care of a few things first," said Andreas.

Then Bettina said her father-in-law had been a wonderful man. She often thought of the last Christmas they had spent together.

"I phoned him about a month before he died," said Andreas. "I meant to visit him, but I left it too late. No one expected him to fade as quickly as he did."

"He was always very pleased when you called."

Andreas said the funeral had been awful. It was like being in a bad film. He hadn't understood what was going on around him.

"I think I was closer to him than I ever realized. I didn't see much of him in his last years, and when I called him I was often stuck for things to say. But then I would see him in the things that I said and did myself."

"He told me once he wished he could have had a life like yours," said Bettina. "You really are like him."

There were steps on the gravel, and Andreas asked Bettina not to mention his illness to Walter. It would only alarm him.

"Do you have someone you can talk to?" asked Bettina.

"Yes," said Andreas. "I think so."

"You know you can come here any time. You can stay with us too, if you can't manage anymore. We've got plenty of room."

"Things aren't that bad yet," said Andreas. "But thank you for offering."

She said she wished he got in touch more often, and he promised to try. He saw her eyes were misting over. When Walter joined them, she turned away.

Andreas said he would go from the cemetery straight back to the hotel. He was leaving tonight. Walter said that was a shame.

Andreas went up to Bettina. She turned and hugged him. Then they all went into the house together. Walter called the children.

"Andreas has to go," he said.

They walked to the cemetery. Andreas asked Walter how he was doing, what he was up to, and Walter started telling him. He told him about the vacation in Sweden that they had just returned from, and a canoeing trip in the rain. He made some comment about good-looking Swedish women. Andreas had never known Walter to be so talkative.

Walter said these might be their last vacations as

a family all together. Even this year, Maia would rather have gone hitchhiking with a girlfriend. Next year she was finishing school, and she might go to France for a few months to learn the language. She had been very taken with Paris, that time they had all descended on Andreas. Lukas had no idea what he wanted to do, but there was plenty of time to decide that. Bettina was thinking of going back to work, with the children out of the house. She was taking a computer course.

"And what about you?" asked Andreas.

"I'm fine," said Walter. "My promotion has changed a few things."

"You never told me."

Walter gestured dismissively. That was a couple of years ago now. He said it wasn't a dream job. He had often thought of doing something else. But with the economy as it was, it wasn't a time to take risks. He imagined he would probably stay with the same firm until he retired. He laughed sheepishly.

"It must all seem terribly boring to you."

"No," said Andreas. "No, it's not boring at all. Sometimes I envy you the children and Bettina. You've got on with your life."

There was no one at the cemetery. Walter made straight for the grave, and Andreas thought he must have

been there many times. Walter knelt down, and plucked
a few twigs from a little bush that grew in front of the
stone.

He didn't mind that the grave was being leveled,
said Andreas. He often thought about his parents, but
his memories of them were attached to the places where
they had lived, not this place where they were buried.
Walter didn't say anything. In all their phone calls over
the years he had never talked about his parents. Nor did
he speak about them now, but just about their grave and
the flowers on it, which he had replanted in the spring,
even though it was really no longer worth it.

They stood in front of the grave in silence. Then
Walter said, Well! as if he had completed a task. His
voice sounded a little less burdened as they picked their
way through the rows of graves and he spoke of one or
another deceased whom they had both known, a school
friend of Andreas's who had died very young in a traffic accident, the proprietress of a haberdashery store,
Walter's former music teacher. They parted company
at the level crossing.

"The next time you come you stay with us," said
Walter. "Will you promise me that?"

Andreas promised.

"And you'll stay for a bit longer?"

"OK."

"Be good, then, and drive safely."

All at once, Andreas believed there would be such a thing as a next time. He quickly hugged his brother, and then they each went their separate ways.

Andreas thought of Delphine, all the moving she had been put through as a child, such that her childhood memories were not attached to any particular place. She had said she could feel at home anywhere. Andreas wondered if that was a fault or a strength in her. Perhaps it would be simpler not to have any roots. It was like scattering the ashes of the dead. They were everywhere and nowhere. Whereas his childhood was just as much buried in this place as his parents were, but when he stood in front of their grave, he didn't see much more than a stone with their names and dates on it. His memories were no more alive there than anywhere else. Only the sense of loss might be greater. Perhaps he shouldn't have gone back—either that or he shouldn't have left, like his brother. Then he might slowly have gotten used to the changes, just as you got used to the changes in your body, and yet seemed to be the same person from your childhood into ripe old age.

In the hotel, he packed his bags. He went down to the front desk and said he was leaving. It took the desk clerk a long time to make out the bill. Andreas took a postcard from a display, five sunny views of the village: the Catholic and Protestant churches, the town hall, the community center, and the steps up to some historic building, where long ago some freedom fighter had given an important speech. At last the clerk had finished adding up the bill, and Andreas put back the postcard and paid.

The easy mood of that morning had left him. Andreas felt tired and confused. He drove off aimlessly, heading west. He had the radio on, a classical music program that was comparing different recordings of the same piece of music. The host talked about the details of the various interpretations with two guests—a male and a female musician. One interpretation was too quick for them, another one dragged. They criticized soloists who made too much of themselves, and others who played with too little expression, or were imprecise, or with a show of feeling. Andreas tried to hear the differences they talked about, but for the most part he couldn't.

The further west he got, the weaker the reception. More and more the music was interrupted by hissing, and then suddenly there was a different station, a French-language pop station, and a couple of excitable DJs who were talking nonsense and kept interrupting each other. Andreas pushed in the cassette that was in the player. It was the language course that he and Delphine had heard on the way here, the kind man who had cheese and sausage for breakfast, and took the bus to work, ate lunch in the cafeteria, where he had a choice of three delicious specials, and then went home at the end of his work.

After supper I sit down in front of the television and watch the news. The evening program is of no great interest to me. Usually, the interesting programs are on too late for me. I like to go to bed early. The night is quickly over. When the alarm clock goes off in the morning, I usually feel I haven't had enough sleep. And the next day follows in the same way.

Andreas stopped at a rest stop. He sat in his car and listened to a man talking about his life. When the sentences stopped, his body cramped, and he started to tremble, as though in a fever. He choked, and then he sobbed, dryly and convulsively. When at last the tears came, he stopped trembling, and became calmer. He dropped his head on the steering wheel, and cried for a long time, not really knowing why.

The tape had kept on playing. When Andreas next heard it, a woman was speaking with strange emphasis.

I hurt myself. You hurt yourself. He hurts himself. We hurt ourselves. You hurt yourselves. They hurt themselves.

He took the tape out of the player. He got out of the car, and walked to the men's room to wash his face. He dropped the cassette into a garbage bin that had thank you written on it in four languages. He sat down at one of the washable concrete picnic tables in the bright sun. When he had calmed down a bit, he drove on.

Fifty miles from Paris, Andreas took the highway west. He thought he had an aerial view of himself driving through the dark landscape, of which he had little sense. For a long time the road led through fields and woods, past scattered villages. Occasionally it brushed a town, and he could read advertisements for cheap hotels and shopping centers. Once, Andreas almost dropped off. His car had slowly drifted into the passing lane, without his noticing. It was only a loud, insistent car horn that woke him out of his dream. He jerked at the steering wheel, and the 2CV yawed off, wobbling wildly, and a car overtook him, so close that they almost brushed each other. Andreas's heart beat wildly. He opened the window. Warm air flowed in, and the cheeping of the crickets was so loud he could hear it over the sound of the engine.

Andreas turned the radio on again. He caught one of his favorite programs, *Du jour au lendemain*, on *France Culture*. The host was interviewing a French writer, whom Andreas had never heard of and who appeared to be quite unreadable. He gave long answers, of which Andreas understood about half, even after he'd closed the window. The writer had once been religious, had even wanted to become a priest, but, having become a creator himself, a writer, he had begun to question God. Now he only believed in the strength of the Self, the life force, which was stronger than any effort, any pain, than even the death that surrounded us all. The life force of every individual was finally stronger than the absolute, sapped its strength, crushed it, brought it to its knees. This Self, upper case, he said. Andreas envied the man's self-confidence. He had never had a very clear sense of himself. Perhaps that was why he had led such a regular life. The monotony of his days had been his only prop. Without a job, without an apartment, without a schedule, his dates with women and appointments with friends were the only fixed points in a menacingly empty landscape.

He thought of the evenings with Nadia, or rather the same evening over and over. Emptiness was repetition, he had thought at the time. But that wasn't right. Emptiness lurked somewhere beyond repetition. Fear of emptiness was fear of disorder, of chaos, of death.

Andreas had wanted to drive all night. But when he saw the signs for motels again, he decided to take a room and rest up for a few hours. The motel was just next to the highway exit. In a convenience store next door, he bought himself a few cans of beer. The motel's front desk was manned by a sleepy North African man, who asked him to pay for the room in advance.

Even though Andreas was tired, he couldn't fall asleep. He drank beer and watched TV until his eyes fell shut. In his dream he was driving. He saw the center median and then he didn't see it, he felt its rhythm like a series of dull blows to his head. The car tumbled into a dark abyss, and the center median flew by and its rhythm accelerated like a drum roll as he fell unstoppably down.

Andreas woke up bathed in sweat and feeling just as tired as when he'd gone to sleep. It was early; dawn was just breaking outside. He took a shower and carried his bags downstairs. There was no one at the desk. There was a card showing the hours breakfast was served, and a number to call in case of emergencies.

Andreas didn't want to waste any time, and he decided to drive on.

As he stowed his suitcase in the trunk, his eye caught the bundle with the hunting goddess statue. He unwrapped it, and ran his fingertips over the gleaming bronze body, the tiny breasts, and the little face, which had always reminded him of Fabienne's, which over the years had come to stand in for Fabienne's face, and which, as he now saw, was nothing like her. He felt the bow and the quiver with the bent wire arrows, the short tunic she wore, the legs frozen in mid-leap, the feet, of which only one touched the base, on tiptoe. He weighed it in his hands. He thought of throwing it away, but instead he wrapped it up again and carefully laid it in the trunk.

At noon he passed Bordeaux. He bought a regional map at a gas station. After looking for some time, he found the campsite that Delphine had told him about, *Le Grand Crohot*. A road led straight into the sea, and ended there. There were no buildings on the map, the only thing there beside the name was the symbol for a view.

The highway cut through pinewoods and low scrub. The traffic was heavy, and when the road got narrower, a few kilometers from the sea, it came to a dead stop. The very last bit of road took Andreas almost an hour. The sun burned down on the car, and he began to sweat.

The road ended in a gigantic loop. At the edge of the road were hundreds of parking spots in the shadow of tall pines. Many of them were occupied, and here and there he could see people in swim suits, unpacking their things or picnicking next to their cars. Andreas drove on, very slowly. After a couple of hundred yards, he reached the entrance to the campsite. The reception area was closed for lunch, and wouldn't open until two. Andreas parked the car and called Delphine on her mobile. She didn't answer. He listened to her recording all the way through, but he didn't leave a message. Presumably Delphine was on the beach and didn't have her phone with her.

Next to the entrance gate was a map of the campsite. There were two hundred spaces, and a couple of dozen little cabins that were marked as brown rectangles on the map. It would take forever to find Delphine, and presumably she was swimming anyway. Andreas decided to go down to the beach, and to come back here later. In the shade of the car, he changed his clothes, put on some sunscreen, and pulled on a T-shirt. Barefoot, he crossed the campsite in the direction where he thought the sea must be. The campsite seemed to be quite full, but he didn't see many people. The few he passed wore casual clothes, tracksuits, shorts and T-shirts, and sandals. At the edge of a great expanse of sand, rimmed by some café tables and chairs, a couple of men were playing boules by themselves. So this was the Paradise that Delphine had raved about: long rows of tents and campers under a canopy of tall pine trees, a food shop and a washeteria, little paved footpaths, and every hundred yards or so a building housing toilets, and another with showers and wash basins. On some of the sites a little tent had been erected next to a big one, on others windbreaks had been put up to shield the occupants from nosy passersby. Hammocks and clotheslines with wet towels hanging from them had been suspended between trees. In front of some of the tents, the pine needles had been raked to little paths, edged on either side by pine cones.

Andreas had always had a horror of campsites. Once, he had agreed to go, and had spent a week in a tent by the Mediterranean with a girlfriend. All he could remember were damp clothes, sand everywhere, stinking toilets, crowded beaches, and dance nights, whose climax was the duck dance. He left the girl shortly afterward, for some reason or other.

Andreas got to the end of the campsite. He had no idea now where the sea was. He wandered about among the trees. Finally, the woods thinned out, and a high dune rose in front of him. He trudged through the hot sand. Only now did he feel how tired he was. Once up at the top, he turned to look back. He could no longer see the campsite, only an endless wood, and, a little way off, a mighty bunker, half sunk in sand. The thick concrete shell had cracked open, and the walls were smeared with graffiti.

He couldn't see the sea from here either, but he could at least hear the sound of the surf. He passed through a narrow cleft, and climbed another few yards. Then he suddenly felt the wind, and saw the sea ahead of him, and below him the beach, which seemed to go on forever in either direction, before losing itself in a yellow haze. The beach was almost entirely deserted. A couple of hundred yards from Andreas, people lay a little more closely packed. Blue flags were stuck in the sand, and a lifeguard sat up on a raised chair. Children stood in the water, young people, parents with children, entire families. They stood close together in knee-deep water, in front of the back and forth of the waves, as though waiting for something to happen. They looked small in the sea, which had no scale. Andreas slithered down the dune. The nearer he got to the sea, the smaller he too seemed to become. He felt very alone, abandoned —a feeling he had often had as a child. He turned south, and away from the blue flags.

There were only a few people dotted about on the sand, bronzed couples, lying side by side or in embraces. One woman lay limply across the back of a man, her legs dangling off to the side, it looked like a failed attempt at some outlandish copulation. The distances between the bathers grew larger. Only here and there did Andreas pass groups of towels and umbrellas that looked like the final outposts of a vanishing civilization. He walked on. From time to time a naked man passed him, and as they crossed, each averted his eyes, as though the meeting was painful or embarrassing to them both. Andreas walked close to the water, where the sand was firm and the waves straightaway erased his traces. Sometimes he walked on a thin sheet of water, that was pulled away from under his feet, until he had the sensation of walking sideways. He turned around and looked behind him. There was no one there, not a sign, not a trace. He took everything off except for his sunglasses, and lay down in the sand. The feeling of solitude had grown weaker, the further he was from the last human. Now it had quite disappeared. He felt as though he himself was no longer human. He lay on his back and looked up at the sky. Its blue was so porous, that he could feel the blackness of space behind it. The wind kept up, and the crashing of the surf was a continuum, the individual waves were not identifiable. You would have to be here for weeks, thought Andreas, sit naked for hours in the sun and the wind, and turn brown, dry out in the salty air, be softened by the blowing sand like driftwood, become tough and resistant. Then nothing more could happen to you. He fell asleep and awoke again. He sat up, and looked down at the water. The sun was low in the sky. The sea had withdrawn a little, the waves were a little lower, but the wind had freshened, and pushed Andreas, drove him on. He shut his eyes. He saw himself and Delphine sitting in a sidewalk café on the Champs-Elysées. What a coincidence, he could hear himself say, and Delphine said: Why didn't you come to the station to see me off? My car broke down, he said. I lost your address. Sentences he remembered reading, it was long ago.

What a coincidence it was that he had met Fabienne, Nadia, Sylvie, and Delphine. That he had gone to Paris, and now come here, to this wide beach. It was coincidence that his parents had met, and before them his grandparents and great-grandparents, however much they might have wanted to think the opposite, however much they might have wanted to persuade themselves that destiny had brought them together. His birth, any birth, was the last of an endless row of coincidences. Only death was no coincidence.

He thought of the chances that had brought him and Delphine together, and separated them again. A sudden shower of rain, a telephone call at the wrong moment, a whim would have sufficed to bring the whole complex edifice of little events and unimportant decisions to a crashing fall.

He got up and headed back. The wind was in his face, and sometimes it was so gusty that it sprayed his face with a fine foam. At the place where he had crossed the dune, he hesitated for a moment, and then walked on, toward the blue flags.

He imagined moving in with Delphine, in Paris or Versailles or wherever. He no longer had any possessions, and she didn't seem to own much either. They would settle in somewhere, buy furniture and kitchen equipment, perhaps a TV and a stereo. He asked himself what they would do with their time, with such time as remained to them. But that didn't matter. He had to find Delphine and speak to her. He had to call the doctor, to pick up the test results, even if they finally didn't mean anything.

There were still quite a lot of people on the beach, but not many in the water. The sun was low over the sea, against the light, the swimmers were only visible as black outlines. Even so, he recognized Delphine immediately. She was standing in the water with her back to him. He shouted to her, but the noise swallowed his voice. He went up to her. The water was cold and murky with spinning sand. He stopped a few yards behind Delphine and watched as, with mechanical movements, she jumped into the waves, got up, took a few steps back, without reason and without end. Sometimes she dropped to her knees, and disappeared into the water, and then she got up again. Finally she turned around and made for him with quick loose strides. She was wearing a flowered bikini, and her body was glistening and wet. Her head was lowered, and she was looking at the water in front of her. It wasn't until she had almost reached Andreas that she noticed him. She said something he couldn't hear, and laughed and kissed him. They hugged each other so tight that it hurt. Delphine's body was cool. Over her shoulder, not far away, Andreas saw another couple embracing, and he felt he was seeing himself and Delphine, as though he were a very long way away from it all. Only the crashing of the waves was very near and held him.